Gatherings IX

The En'owkin Journal of
First North American Peoples

Beyond Victimization:
Forging a Path to Celebration

Fall 1998

Theytus Books Ltd.
Penticton, BC, Canada

Gatherings
The En'owkin Journal of First North American Peoples
Volume IX 1998

Canadian Cataloguing in Publication Data
Main entry under title:
Gatherings

Annual.
ISSN 1180-0666

1. Canadian literature (English)--Indian authors--Periodicals.
2. Canadian literature (English)--20th century--Periodicals. 3.
American literature--Indian authors--Periodicals. 4. American
literature--20th century--Periodicals. I. En'owkin International
School of Writing. II. En'owkin Centre.
PS8235.I6G35   C810.8'0897   CS91-031483-7

Editor:	Greg Young-Ing
Assistant Editor:	Graham Proulx
Technical Editor:	Rasunah Marsden
Design & Layout:	Marlena Dolan
Proof Reading:	Regina (Chick) Gabriel
Cover Design:	Marlena Dolan
Cover Art:	Lisa Hudson

Please send submissions and letters to *Gatherings*, c/o En'owkin Centre,
RR #2, Site 50, Comp. 8, Penticton, BC, V2A 6J7, Canada. All submissions
must be accompanied by a self-addressed envelope (SASE). Manuscripts
without SASE's may not be returned. We will not consider previously
published manuscripts or visual art.

*The publisher acknowledges the support of the Canada Council, Department of
Canadian Heritage and the Cultural Services Branch of the Province of British
Columbia in the publication of this book.*

Printed in Canada

Table of Contents

Introduction

I was an aspiring writer fresh out of university in 1990. That was the year I had some work published in the first volume of *Gatherings: The En'owkin Journal of First North American Peoples* published by Theytus Books. I vividly recall the excitement running through the Aboriginal writers community about the first journal in North America that would publish a current sampling of Aboriginal literature each year.

The following year, I was asked to be Managing Editor of Theytus Books. Though I was young and inexperienced , I could not turn down the challenge of working with the first Aboriginal owned press in Canada. And so I could scarcely believe it when I found myself Editor of *Gatherings Volume II* in 1991 and *Volume III* in 1992. After that we decided to approach different Aboriginal writers and/or teachers to edit the journal each year.

Thanks to Jeannette Armstrong, Linda Jaine, Don Fiddler, Beth Cuthand, Kateri Akiwenzie-Damm, Joyce Joe, William George, Susan Beaver, and the many others who have volunteered their time and talent toward the editorial effort required to compile this journal each year. Many thanks also to the hundreds of Aboriginal writers who have contributed their work over the years.

In this ninth volume, we have sought submissions under the theme "Beyond Victimization: Forging a Path of Celebration." Aboriginal Peoples have much to celebrate. Our ceremonies, literature, stories, songs, dances and cultural traditions, are all testimony of nations steeped in pride, strength and forbearance. Through cultural celebration, we enable ourselves to respond positively to the issues of the day—thus empowering the agenda of achieving appropriate cultural, political and legal recognition. We hope this theme has produced a volume that encompasses a wide range of literary approaches.

Here in 1998, after publishing eight volumes of *Gatherings* and over fifty titles, I find myself once again at the editorial helm of another volume of the journal, as we look back and ponder the prospect of celebrating one decade of *Gatherings* next year.

Greg Young-Ing,
Managing Editor

Enduring

A Sister Flies Ahead of Me Now
(For EK (Kim) Caldwell 1954-1997)

I discover you
not unlike the way Columbus
supposed he had discovered us;
you were already there . . . settled,
imposing, beautiful, shining in the light
of morning.

We sit, reeking of sage,
flying to gather in the Oneida woods.
In the old way of asking, we find
each other sisters in the family circle
of word weavers, of story singers,
of water bearers.

Your smiles collect
on my shoulders and my ears ring
with your words. We are women,
satisfied to sit with our saged-up bodies
and learn each other. We have husbands,
write poems to stay alive, love being brown.
I know you a thousand days by the end
of our five hour flight.

Now you fly overhead;
I cup my eyes, shadow the sun to see you;
yesterday I caught a breath of sage
in the grocery store, thought you might
be there buying oranges or bread for dinner.
I walk past the waft of memory; hear you chuckle.
I buy the oranges and bread myself,
crying and laughing and getting a new poem.

Carol Snow Moon Bachofner

My sage is safe in the Eagle bag you gave me
when we met. You are there too in the twist
of red cloth, in the pocket of my coat where
my hand can touch your gift. Fire and I send
sparks of prayers to where you fly. You are
a brown, round woman of the air, circling me
and giving me new songs to sing, new words
to weave. So how can I begin to miss you?

Give Us The Stars & The Moonlight
for Mary TallMountain

when you left us we remembered
    your steady words, your strong spirit

your words about the land & people you were taken from
    when you were young

we remembered your spirit
that so often rose up high in the sky
    and carried us over every sharp peak
every deep abyss

you saved us, Mary Tallmountain
Mary TallMountain
you saved us with your words & songs & dreams
    about our Native America
your Alaskan, Athabaskan birthplace

Mary, give us this day
give us the stars & the moonlight
    the sunlight fierce, the ocean winds blowing
the shine in your eyes, still present
    in every blinking streetlight
    in every busy storefront window
in this sometimes foggy
    sometimes sunny
vibrant city that was your home for so many years—
Mary,
San Francisco,
your urban tenderloin,
misses you.

Where I Come From

where i come from
people are not afraid
    to fight
not afraid
    to speak up & speak out
to challenge injustice.

where i come from
people love
    join together & help one another
sometimes argue, sometimes fight each other
    but remember
to make peace with each other
    remember
who the real enemy is.

where i come from
people struggle
    people are poor
people don't always have enough to eat
    enough clothes to wear
but people share.

where i come from
people dare to be different
    dare to begin revolutions
    dare to sing & dance
    dare to love
dare to love.

where i come from
people make music
    with the wind, trees, earth
and drum.

wide open fields & sunny blue skies are where i come from
where i come from.

dry canyons & raging rivers are where i come from
where i come from.

mountains of snow & lakes of ice are where i come from
where i come from.

red earth
red earth
a land so dark & giving
        is where i come from
where i come from.

IN OKLAHOMA

in oklahoma, it's said
the civil war never died.

in oklahoma, we watch
right-wing reactionaries
white cloaked reactionaries
    murder
    blow up
babies, young children
mothers, fathers, families
of all races, all colours.

in oklahoma, how easy it is to kill
in oklahoma, how easy it is to forget
    whose land you're on
    the trail of tears
150 years of indian deaths
indian lives that never mattered to the ruthless land-robbers
to the hateful colonizers of oil-rich indian lands.

In oklahoma, we never knew your green hills
    and blue spring skies
would be darkened by the ash & smoke
of a megaton bomb.

we never knew
your young & old & hardworking & poor
would die in a flash
of hatred, revenge
and death—
we never knew.

In oklahoma we never knew how many
would suffer
    would lose
their children, loved ones, friends

in oklahoma, we never knew
that yesterday's land wars and murder of indian young
        would come back to haunt
your blue skies.

we never knew the civil war never died
    in oklahoma

and somehow we forgot how
modern-day terrorists
like yesterday's terrorists
never hesitate to kill ...

What We Are Not

They walk alone
in fear of everything
They compete with one another,
for power and material things.
They respect nothing,
consider nobody
but themselves.

Their fate is tragedy
their selfishness breeds hatred.
Their divided nations
created instability
and isolation.
Their future will
prove them wrong.

They oppress other nations
they dominate our world
They create laws that
limit our movement
They impose sanctions
which halt our successes.
They tell us "no,"
as if we were children
We are not.

Untitled

Tonight
is the night
of fire

of fire
sage
and eagle
feathers

tonight
I crawl
through ceremony
sage
and stars

I scream
and scream
again
the names
of those who have
desecrated my body
my soul

I scream at the moon
for revenge
justice

you did not have to go
to a residential school
to suffer hell

I did not go to a residential shool
it came to me

Chris Bose

but tonight
as I stand
in a forest
in the mountains
I take it all back

one song
one ceremony
one night
at a time

and there is nothing
you can do about it.

There Are No Vanished Tribes

storm clouds migrate in my direction, arms outstretched as if to embrace me in the manner of words. i sit, an anxious mother waiting for her children to return after a long absence. they come home in the shape of gray blue bodies crawling down the mountains outside a bed i chose as my own. the songs returning home have been contorted through centuries of abuse, lungs clawed at by steel jaws, torn away in their youth then left for dead in clear-cut forests and diverted rivers.

words and song slip off the tongue of crow. she feeds those of us still alive, sliding her beak down our throats, replacing starvation with the voices caught on the breath of millennium. words and song fill my stomach drowning my heart in resistance my mouth wide open they leave in their wake a trail for others yet to come. they have survived and have come home to me, illuminated in translucent light, knowing they have not been numbered amongst the missing. in my belly a ghost dance of tone and rhythm is taking place. only outsiders believe in vanished tribes, between my joints they are still living. they dance within pregnant clouds. they roam inside my house, filling my rooms with conversation and laughter.

i watch as they throw off their cloaks of starvation and disease, discarding half truths and broken promises. they are planning a revolt and scream revolution at the slow rising red moon, chanting, calling me home. their blood is seen roaming across horizons yet to be formed. they call *come home, come home, understand the moment is now*. they whisper *listen to the movement within your ribcage*, words, song, vanished tribes crawl out from beneath rocks. they slither into the palm of tomorrow. spitting into the earth they birth revolution. words, song, vanished tribes housed in stones voice slide down my throat. they murmur *the moment is now.*

Connie Fife

storm clouds migrate home
   i sit an anxious mother
waiting for her children to return
   following their absence

they return in the shape of words and song
   filling my house with conversation and laughter
vanished tribes crawl inside my stomach
   where a ghost dance has almost finished

crow has filled my belly
   with the tone and rhythm of revolution
while overhead the moon slowly rises
   as blood flows down her cheeks

Loaves and Fishes

Manna Redpaint forages for food. She tears through the card-board boxes of *Tide* under the sink, sending sandy powder across the tile floor. A box of *Brillo* contains only *Brillo* pads. Manna hurls the pads over her slim shoulder.

Gallup has been cruel to Manna. She hitched a ride here from Cherokee, North Carolina, fled here with a fancy dancing stranger. She meant to escape her domineering mother and to forget a flute player named Thomas Crow. Instead, Manna Redpaint has hunger pains, indigo bruises and a baby—a toddler really—left behind by one of the stranger's drinking pals. She is forgetting what it is like to eat from all four food groups in the same day.

"Russian roulette," Manna Redpaint says to no one in particu-lar. She drums her slender fingers against the once-white of the refrigerator. "Open the door—there's food—we live. There's not . . ." Manna Redpaint bites the inside of her golden cheek. She shuts her eyes and wraps her hand around the handle.

Manna Redpaint opens the refrigerator. The bulb lights timid-ly. One egg sits forlornly among thirteen red and white cans of *Budweiser*. Manna, who already has teeth and bones strong enough for all practical purposes, gave the last of the milk to the baby yes-terday. She prays that calcium is cumulative.

Loaves and fishes gone haywire, Manna muses. Good sign. If she can joke, her mind must be working. As long as she can think, she can create a solution, stay one hunger pang ahead of starvation. Manna rubs her black hair between her hands. The sound makes Manna feel like a Scout, setting forests aflame with friction.

Manna opens the cupboard again, removing only a plastic compact. No crumpled portraits of Thomas Jefferson fall from the layers of pressed powder. The compact clatters into the sink. Fragile grains float into the ever-present drip of water and disap-pear. Lifting the smooth compact, Manna Redpaint drops it again. It clatters against the chrome, losing slices of powder.

"No! No! No!" Manna roars. She strikes the sink with the side of her hand. The compact leaps, landing with a shattering sound. Glass slivers shower her waist, scatter over her knuckles, as the lid surrenders. Tiny droplets of blood flow crimson over her fingers.

17

Manna reaches for a dishtowel, wincing at its sourness. She turns on the faucet. Her own blood floods away with dust of opal powder. Shaking her hand free of blood and water, Manna wraps it in the dishrag.

Manna's blood produces no miracles. The baby is standing in the doorway, watching. Her peaked face convicts Manna, who has been crushing compacts and feeling sorry for herself instead of feeding her. Manna wipes her wet eyes with her good hand.

"Oh Baby, I am so sorry." The baby stares at Manna. Her eyes widen as she notices the blood seeping onto Manna's skirt through the dishrag.

"Hurt?"

"Honey, it's just scratches. It hurts a whole lot more on the inside than on the out.

"Ouch?"

"Yes, ouch, but not too bad. I'm sorry if I scared you." She is not only letting this child starve into the next world, but terrifying her in the process. "My temper got away from me for a minute, but I chased it down and brought it back." Another joke. She has not lost her entire mind. "I'm fine, honey, Manna's okay."

"Mama, okay?"

Manna has no idea. She can hardly keep up with her own hunger pangs and breaking mirrors and worry about this baby's missing mother at the same time.

"I don't know, sweet pea. I don't even know who Mama is. But I'm fine. Manna's fine."

The baby considers this gravely. "Mama okay." She smiles at Manna, who realizes that her tiny jaw is moving. Chewing.

"Is there something in your mouth?"

The baby nods.

"Are you eating?"

Another nod. Food. Manna hopes that whatever it is, it's non-toxic and plentiful. She forces calmness into her voice as she reaches for the child.

"Can you show me what you're eating?"

Nodding again, the baby draws a sheet of paper from behind her small back. The paper is the colour of tired goldenrods. The corners and a fair part of the middle are missing.

"Oh good Lord." Manna's heart grows more exhausted by the minute. The baby places the paper in Manna's palm. "Thank you, honey." Manna closes her weak fingers around the coloured paper. She hopes that paper can be considered fibre. Maybe there are minerals in the dye. The baby swallows. Manna's head hurts.

An Eagle and the profile of a Dog Soldier sprawl across the sheet. The title of the event is missing, but the baby has been gracious enough not to eat the date or the location.

"The VA . . ." Manna reads the date again. Tonight, in downtown Gallup. "It's probably a powwow or something for veterans," she tells the baby, who grasps the flyer. Manna holds if out of her reach.

"Hold your horses, little lady. If this is what I think it is, you might not have to eat paper after all. They have fry bread at powwows and we're pretty or pitiful enough to get somebody to give us some. Might even throw in some sweet red *Kool-Aid*." The baby lunges toward the paper. Manna continues to read.

"Mama!" shouts the baby.

Manna's eyes find slim letters at the bottom of page. *Admission: 2 canned goods*. Canned goods. If people gave canned goods, they'd need someone to get them. Manna catches her breath at the promise of pasteurized heaven.

"Food!" Manna clasps the flyer. For food, for canned goods, they can walk far enough to hitch a ride in town and the VA. "Canned goods!" Manna drops to her knees in front of the baby.

"We are going to get cleaned up and go get our fair share of food, little lady." Inspired, Manna squeezes the small body. "We may even take them a few cans of our own."

Manna kisses the baby and heads for the fridge.

Manna and the baby know how to wait. They sit patiently beside the road. Manna feels less like a bad example of hitchhiking since they are only doing it to find food. Besides, they are going to a powwow full of veterans, who have to be better role models than the staggering partiers that surrounded the baby earlier.

The VA is a good place for the baby. If the flyer fails them, she will leave the baby there. Veterans like babies. TV news always shows them rescuing infants from firefights and carrying toddlers piggyback toward democracy. A veteran may keep the baby or find someone who can prevent a mission school or Mormon from claiming her tiny soul. Maybe an elderly woman will raise her to replace a daughter she lost years ago. If the flyer lies, if there is no food, Manna will observe the old women, looking for one who dances Southern cloth and laughs at the M.C.'s jokes.

"If there is no food, I will give you up," Manna whispers into the baby's ear. "Promise you will not starve." The baby sighs and sucks on the fringe of Manna's dance shawl. Manna has had enough. A struggling mother and child may not halt the sporadic traffic, but unattended *Budweiser* is another story.

Manna leaves a six-pack in the middle of the desolate highway. In minutes, the driver and passenger of a red Ford pickup stop to claim the windfall of apparently deserted beer. When they pull away, they don't notice that Manna and the baby have made themselves small in the bed of the vehicle. When they arrive in the VA parking lot, they have no way of knowing that, every so often, spirits are currency.

"These are not canned goods."

The woman guarding the door to the VA glares over her glasses. She is odd angles and wrinkles, the colour of newsprint. She thrusts her hands deep into the pockets of her denim dress.

"Ma'am?" Manna shifts the baby to her other hip. Her eyes meet the woman's and holds them. After a lifetime of her mother's withering stare, it will take more than a scowl to deter Manna from her pursuit of packaged food.

"I said," the woman says sharply, "these are not canned goods." Manna pities the white woman for defending the door instead of enjoying the powwow.

"Ma'am," Manna speaks slowly. "These are canned goods. Goods in cans. B-Vitamins, yeast, all pasteurized even."

Manna points to the sheet of golden paper on the table, next to a box of creased one-dollar bills and VA information pamphlets.

"Your own flyer says two canned goods per person for admission to this powwow. We have six cans here." Manna taps a can in time with beat of the drum inside. "That's six cans in exchange for me and a baby, who really should be one canned good in the first place." Manna waves her own flyer, creating a slight breeze across the baby's face. The baby reaches for the fan-paper, and Manna lets her have it. "You're almost making a profit here."

"This is a *sobriety* powwow." The woman stretches "sobriety" into a snake of sinister syllables. "*Sobriety* is practised here."

"Well, I can appreciate that, Ma'am. But you see the title of the event is missing from our flyer. I didn't know." Manna Redpaint smiles sweetly. "Both the baby and I are sober."

Pursing her lips in disapproval, the gray lady frowns. "Two canned goods or five dollars." Her eyes narrow as she stares at the baby. "Is your daughter eating that paper?"

"Oh, God. Honey give that here." Manna envies the baby's goat stomach. She feels cruel, demanding that the baby spit out her only sure source of nourishment. She squeezes the baby's cheeks. The baby continues to chew.

"Ma'am, we don't have five dollars. We don't have any dollars. To tell you true, all we have is this beer here and we don't even drink and we're . . ." The baby swallows the paper. Manna leans over the table and whispers.

"We're hungry."

Inside the VA, drums are playing a sneak-up. Manna misses her Cherokee, misses the Ceremonial Grounds, longs for the sight of Thomas Crow in the powwow area. She should never have fled to Gallup to starve, trying to make miracles out of spirits. The baby bites into the paper again. Manna does nothing to stop her.

The woman looks at the baby and turns to talk to Manna.

"Maybe if you spent your welfare check on *food* instead of liquor," she pronounces it lick-or, giving the word a self-righteous sound, "you and your daughter would not go hungry enough to eat paper." Manna's face burns. She straightens, raises her chin. "We are hungry, now. We will not always be hungry. But you, will always be narrow-minded and mean."

Manna snatches several sheets of paper from the table. She hands them to the baby. Gesturing, the woman opens her mouth in protest.

"Blessed is she who gives paper to the poor," Manna tells her. Then she carries the beer and the baby away from the VA.

Someone is shouting at Manna. Manna stands straight, ignores the noise, figures it must be the woman, demanding her flyers. Manna crosses the parking lot, heading for the road. The baby rings Manna's neck with her chubby arms.

"Hey lady," a teenager grabs Manna's upper arm. Red fringe rises and falls as he moves. A grass dancer. He grins at Manna, showing egg-white teeth.

"My uncle there, he wants to pay for you two to get in. He heard them give a hard time and he gave them money for you guys, too." The grass dancer points with his lips, motioning toward the VA.

Manna sees a peanut butter-coloured man sitting in a wheelchair. Pewter hair flows over his shoulders, stopping about a column of coloured ribbons. The teenage grass dancer nods at her.

"He ain't no crazy, lady, he's a veteran. Vietnam, but he's okay. What do you want to carry? The beer or the baby?" Manna hands him the beer. "Okay. Come on. Powwow time for you guys after all."

"Thank you, God," Manna whispers. She looks up, winks at the sky. When her eyes find the earth again, the man in the wheelchair is waving at her. Manna waves back, promising herself that once she has eaten, she will jingle dance and sidestep wildly, to every veteran's honour song.

The Trade

"Eunice, Eunice," louder this time. "Come into my office this instant!"

I looked up from my desk, as did everyone else. I could see his round belly move up and down as he shouted *that* name. His big blue eyes peered over the rim of his small dark frames and his fat finger pointed to the back of the classroom. All students' heads turned and their eyes were on me. But I was not Eunice. My name was not Eunice.

"Stand up," he demanded. My cheeks filled with fire. My legs didn't feel like a part of my body, yet I managed to stand and cling to my desk. Words I barely heard, came from my dry throat, "I'm not Eunice. My name's not Eunice."

Why do you keep calling me that name? I grew to hate the sound of it, I asked the question to myself.

"What's that?" His voice echoed off the chalkboards. "Speak up girl, make yourself clear and stand up straight."

I couldn't stand up straight and I couldn't look into his eyes, so I looked past the staring students, past the scary principal and out the window. My eyes rested on a small brown bird flapping its wings preparing to fly away.

"Eunice . . . pay attention, speak when you're spoken to."

"It's not Eunice." I heard my own voice say. "My name is Janice."

He cleared his throat and adjusted his tie that was squeezing his red neck.

"Oh, so it is. It doesn't change things though. Into my office now . . . Janice." He dragged my name on his tongue. "What you have done is serious young lady, and you will pay the penalty." His fat finger pointed to the door of the room that held the thick, black leather strap. My own fingers were pulling and twisting the sleeve of my woollen sweater. The whole sweater was suddenly itchy and prickly all over. I was sweating, my mouth was like sandpaper and I was scared. But I followed him into the room where only the bad kids went, and the kids that were just different. I was different, I was Indian and now I was a bad Indian. I could feel all eyes searing my back.

"She did it. Kathy saw her. She's awful. She did it." I heard the whispers. Then the snickers.

"Eunice, Eunice, Eunice." It was like hissing. She's worse than those Pettch girls." The words felt hotter and more prickly than my woollen sweater. I bit my bottom lip to stop it from quivering and my teeth held it there until it almost bled. The only ones not snickering were the Pettch girls.

The heavy door opened and closed slamming behind me. The silence in his office was pressing against my ears and making them hurt. He motioned for me to sit in the large black leather chair. I sat, not moving. My feet hung in mid-air, they could not reach the floor. I wished the chair would swallow me entirely. I watched him pull open his desk drawer and place the thick black piece of leather on top of the desk. Then he removed his jacket, undid his shiny silver cuff links and rolled up his shirt sleeves. He did not look at me when he spoke. We both watched his fat hairy fingers move up and down the black leather strip.

"Eunice . . . er, Janice. We don't tolerate *thievery* in this school. I can call the truant officer in, or we can deal with it here, now. You will be taught your lesson. Stealing is a crime." He rubbed the strap some more. "Indian kids need proper direction, if they are to make something of themselves. Now, I want to explain this, and don't try to lie about this. Kathy Anderson saw you hiding these things. These have been stolen from the students here and there are other things missing, too." He opened his desk again and placed a gold pen, two red barrettes, a striped ball and a blue wallet with a pink dancing lady on it in front of me. "Now why don't you start with the right words to explain why this stuff was found in *your* desk!"

His words swirled in a fog making me dizzy. I clutched my stomach. I felt like I was going to throw up. *Thief. I am a thief.* What is he saying to me and why is the pen, the barrettes, ball and the wallet on his desk? They were given to me, in fair trade . . . and then I thought of the Pettch girls.

The Pettch girls. The poor, dirty Pettch girls. No one liked them. No one played with them. They smelled and their clothes were dirty. Their short red hair was tangled and had cooties more than once. Everyone stayed away from the Pettch girls. Of course,

24

everyone stayed away from me too. But I was Indian, that was different. They were not. But they were poor and had dirty, old clothes. I never played with them and they never played with me. But they hung around the school yard together. They had each other. Some days I watched them laughing and sharing jokes, they didn't need anyone or anything. Until last week.

The younger Pettch girl with the dark brown tights, that were so small the crotch hung to her knees, approached me at lunchtime. I wondered how she could walk in those tights. She smelled of stale urine and when she smiled her teeth were yellow. She stood there eyeing my lunch. Though my own clothes were hand-me-downs, and my family was poor, I always had good lunches. Moose meat on bannock, corn soup and fresh berries.

The girl kept her hands behind her back when she spoke, "Wanna trade?" Trade? Trade for what? I thought. I have nothing to trade.

"Wanna trade?" she said again. "A sandwich for this shiny gold pen." She produced a pen from behind her back. The pen was nice, but I wanted my sandwich. I was embarrassed and so was she. And I was hungry, so was she.

"My sis and I are going to share your sandwich," she mumbled.

I shuffled my moose bannock, she shuffled her too tight shoes on her feet. I had my pride, I didn't want her pen. But she had her pride too. I took the pen, she took my sandwich.

The next day at lunch, her bigger sister approached me. She smelled of old underarms and her small blouse was squeezing her breasts, too large for her age. "Wanna trade?" She held out two red barrettes and an Indian rubber, striped ball. The barrettes were nice, the ball I could play with a lot. I wanted my sandwich, but I took the ball and the barrettes. She took the sandwich and my soup. I put the things in my desk. Tomorrow I would keep my own lunch, maybe put in an extra apple or orange and just give it to them.

They never approached me to trade again. In fact, they were both missing from school for days. I was relieved and curious about their absence all the same time. I wrote with the gold pen, played with the Indian rubber ball and kept the barrettes for a special occasion. They were nice things to own. But I didn't want to trade anymore.

Then they were back again. This time both Pettch girls stood before me. They had bruises on them. The bigger girl had bruises on her cheek and the younger one had them on her bare arms.

"Wanna trade, your whole lunch this time?" The younger girl pulled something from her waist and out of her tights. It was the most beautiful blue wallet I had ever seen. The dancer on the wallet was dressed in pink and had ribbons and flowers in her hair. She wore pink satin shoes. I liked the wallet, I could eat when I got home. The Pettch girls probably couldn't. I gave them my whole lunch. I put the wallet in my desk.

"Eunice, ... Janice, whatever ..." He slammed his fist onto the desk. "Explain these stolen items now. I will not wait a moment longer with your stubborn, insolent attitude. You Indian kids act like you're quiet and shy, but don't think I haven't heard the loud whooping sounds you kids make, when you want to." He rolled up his sleeves higher and picked up the black leather strap. "Last chance to confess what you have done wrong, and if you do, maybe we will make you sit in front of the class instead of this." He shook the strap at me.

I stared without emotion. But disbelief and dread filled my insides. In front of the class. Sit in front of the class. Or the thick black belt . . . should I tell him my story. My bottom lip started to bleed from my teeth marks. Only bad kids and different kids were sent to his office. Most of them came out crying or about to. He wouldn't believe that I didn't steal those things. And nobody liked the Pettch girls, and they already had bruises. It wouldn't change anything, no one would still play with me, even if I didn't steal those things. He stood up. He looked like he had grown. "You are defying me." He was mad. "Sitting in front of the class is too easy for you. This will not be tolerated. I will see to it that it is stopped. You Indian kids can be nothing but trouble."

"Eunice ... stand up. Hold out your hand." I had to grab onto the arm of the large leather chair to steady myself. I held out my hand. "My name's not Eunice. It's Janice," I said, over the sound of the smacking black leather.

turtle island holocaust

we have walked on wet stones
to cross a river
and not fallen

we have lived on stone ice and swamp
waiting for your systems to return our stolen land
and been kicked into the stinking gutters of your courts
for offences that have never matched
the atrocities you have committed
on us and this earth
under the banner of civilization
we have been herded into freight trains to nowhere
under the seals of your absent kings and queens
then been dumped dying in snowbanks
covered only by the thin blanket of your diseased integrity
and our will to survive
we have been stripped naked
in your places of worship
and walked away
to watch the sun rise over sacred mountains

we have had our children stolen
so they could be taught to love jesus
white skin the missionary position
and housework
we have lived in the shadow of military invasion
and thrown eggs against your tanks
we have suffered your rocks bullets screwdrivers
we have sung our mourning songs
to young boys with thin necks stretched under leafless trees
their half dressed bodies frozen on roadsides
their mouths wrapped around gun barrels
young girls with arms like pin cushions convulsing in empty buildings
slicing at their memories with razor blades
or eating pills by the bottle
and never waking

we have found our babies
with brains splattered

Kateri Akiwenzie-Damm

hearts stopped dead
bodies burnt to ash

we have endured all this and more

so spare us the burden of your guilt
take your useless pity
your pink-cheeked impotent shame
and drown it in the mercury poisoned water of our rivers

take it
still suckling
from your breast
and throw it naked
on a dark silent slab of concrete

slice its tongue in two
cut its hair with dull scissors
then with european precision
peel its skin from its shivering body
and make a lampshade
to shield us from your thoughts

Inside the House, a Dream

Mud-crusted boots slump by the back steps.

The cold hand of a north wind slams the door shut behind me. Inside, the walls are damp with steam and breath. I pull off my jacket and toque. The warm air leaves beads of sweat and moisture on my skin. My hair is as slick as a newborn's.

Joan.

She stands before me, looking like an elastic stretched to the breaking point. A snake coils around my throat. Another around my chest. My sister doesn't ask if there are partridge or duck hanging in a burlap sack outside. She doesn't ask if there will be venison stew or roast bear or moose nose. She doesn't ask.
She doesn't ask. Anything.
A rat is crawling under my skin.

We stand staring at each other. Time coils and springs, screams, and is silent.

. . . it's Kayly . . .

My niece. These eyes strain in their sockets reaching for Joan's face. The whole world tilts towards her and holds its breath. I tie myself to a tree and wait.

Her breath is thin and slow like a high pitched note. She pushes the words out on top of it.

. . .she was

raped. . .

A snake pit opens in my belly. I puke up hissing questions. Who was it? WHO?

a teacher, her teacher . . .

Where is he? Hunting rifle is jerked up. Shells, pocket. Shells. Shells.

The school? My feet punch the groaning floor.

In the living room I twist like a bear in a leg trap. A gale wind is howling. Waves are sent crashing into rocks, slamming onto the shore. In the living room my voice is an owl screeching his name.

My sister has lost her eyelids. Her lower jaw is unhinged.

I

WILL

KILL

HIM.

The gun barrel crosses my chest like a promise. The wind strips limbs from trees, picks up stones and smashes them to the ground, throws birds into walls, pulls boats down.

I punch a hole in the floor with my heel. Punch the floor. Punch the floor.

Kayly.

Kayly is shivering in the doorway. Everything about her is a question.

Kayly?

The rifle disappears, turns to flesh and bone, becomes an arm held out to her. Two arms that enfold her. We cry and she folds into me, like a fetus into a fetus. I hug her to my belly. Put my arm over her like a shelter, my arm and shoulder forming a rooftop to hold out the rain. My ribs, my flesh and bone and skin form walls to hold out the wind.

Snakes can't cross the threshold.

Safe inside,   we hold each other,   singing lullabies.

Passing Seasons

My childmind remembers
The memory grows like a tree he planted.
Running from memory.
Memory of the evil of fathers
only visited on by daughters.
Memories of stolen innocence.
You are the blackhole of fault
living in the lower intestinals of a gutter rat.
You built these chains of hate
and put me on the rim of a volcano.

Now
I look outside
into the darkness
of midnight,
I think of him.
Walls of fear
surround my heart.
So I sit alone
in the attic of my mind.
But . . .
Deep inside
He can't see inside

There is something inside
Very far inside
Just
a little light
Almost
a smile.

As the season's change
so have the memories.
Once an open, crusted, puss wound,
it has now healed into a fine, thin scar
characterization
of me.

The real me
that *he* can't reach.
As the sun shines,
the birds go on singing,
and the cherry tree blossoms
my smile grows
with passing seasons.

sun baked grass

1

rolling around
in the grassy
playing fields
eyes squinting
cheeks flushed
feet so hot
and every one
hugging
trying
to catch breath
after capturing
soccer game glories

walking home
with Jenn
my little sister
and hanging out
with mom
in the shadiness
of the big tree
outside the window
"one hour till supper"
mom says
so Jenn
and I scramble
outside
running to
the park
to play
in the sun
and the grass
so hot it is steaming
grass dark green
fresh cut
damp and sticking
to my legs
as we run
in the grass

that smells so strong
it gives me a headache
later mom
whistles louder
than eagles shriek
and off we
go back home

2

thirteen is a hard time
to be alive
especially if it is winter
and you're the co-child
of an alcoholic mother
on welfare
as an older child
please be sure to
practice motherhood
on Jennie

make Kraft dinner
or find 30 different
ways to cook potatoes
tuck her in
read her stories
about a girl
named Ramona & her
older sister & their
two parents
read her stories that send her to sleep
wake Jenn up
and pour her corn flakes
do her hair
walk her to school
go to high school

skip school
steal shoes
get caught
given 25 community
hours at the SPCA
taking kittens

to the truck to be *put down*
go home
sidestep puke
take Jennie to the park
away from smoke
away from beer
away from taunting words
& stinky breath
to the park
where suddenly
grass smells so sweet

3

moving from town to city to town
on my own
wondrin' if
any place
where I pay the rent
will ever feel like
home
instead of feeling
so temporary
so wandering nomadic
will I ever stop
feeling like I
abandoned Jenn?
will I ever feel
needed like I did
back home?
thinking now
it's funny
how I don't feel
so deep pressed
in my chest
when I can
smell that
sun baked grass

this generation

centuries ago contagion blew from the ocean and spread across this land
the community bled
many generations bled silently
tap half a drumbeat
sick and during the trek many never made it the whole way
those remembered heartbeats pulse still

this generation bleeds and gaping wounds
within them are pieces felt m i s s i n g or out of reach
them neither present after battle (theirs) nor known to have been killed or
wounded or captured
injury is this deliberate blow for

ad just ment   **transition**   **transportation**

is change possible for the people for the city for the world?
at this time?
in the foreground
in the forest   grows
in the mountains   grows
in the city   grows dissension

drips   trickles   seeps
        oozes   percolates   soaks

immovable massive boulders are levelled to dust in the late 20th century

this generation
dis-arranged   **dislodged**

        dislocated
leaves one distanced from the many

indian here can i be indian anywhere?

MOVE-MENT move a movement has taken place and continues
that contagion's force has diminished and the community's resiliency is
the strength of the people

dream the old dream dream back the stories the language the songs and
add new dreams

survival has changed because it was forced to change
walk the path this generation
this our breath to breathe
we live-move through this world
and our vital participation will contribute to maintaining this changing
landscape

Confronting

Me again

Hello there
its me again
I come before you
   now
in   a vision
a   dream

this is a warning

I am warning you
that
I am coming
and
this time
I will not be content

to   stay in
pemmican/salmon-soaked stories
in teepees
 wigwams
   winterlodges
     and
longhouses

THIS MEANS WAR

and this means that
I will invade you
and
your life
and everything you hold
close
to your heart
like never before

but

Chris Bose

don't take this all so seriously
because
I am joking
I am the trickster
I come before you now
in the
shape of a dream
consider yourself lucky
this time

because

I could come before
you
in the shape of coyote
a raven
a crow
or even an owl

but

you wouldn't want
to see me
          then

I would scare
          you
          to death
and I know you
          wouldn't like that

so beware

I am coming
and I will
          take you
this is war
          these are the lines
this is how it will
end.

Excerpt From Work in Progress
What the Auntys Say
I

there's a fiction between us and them
is what the auntys say
at their schools they call it history
headlines in their news
what they call clearcut
all those mountain hiking boots lined up in a row
hup-two-three-four
hup-two-three-four and feeling like part of the group
sing long and loud in three-part harmony
a logging we will go
a logging we will go
high-ho the dairy-oh
a logging we will go
what they call forest management
reforestation
signs along the roads
crews of planters pioneers
macho whitetown's last frontier
payment by the tree
keeps the kid in university
holy crow and sweat upon the brow
of empty eyes and designer shorts
which makes it worth the work
there's ebb and then there's flow
singing long and singing glee
there were trees
trees
as big as knobby knees
in the store
in the store
there were trees
trees
as big as knobby knees
in the corner master store

II

that round brown face
under a fresh foundation
put there by her foster mother's hand the hand that beats her
yes we've been abused says her foster mothers
the hand that ties those dead chickens around her neck
leaves them there for days
as women we experience sexism
the hand that feeds her slop with bluegreen spots
just before the hogs get the rest
as we get older we encounter ageism
the hand that controls electric fences keeps her in the yard
white picket fences face the road
dupes the neighbours dupes them all
yes says her foster mothers yes
we develop feelings for all the little heathens we raise up
for extended periods of time
rifle cocked and aims right for her godless little heart
that's just before she chases the little slut out the front door
and down to the welfare office
we all have to be careful with our time around here
says that woman at the welfare office
we all have to make room for the other poor children
children much worse off than you my dear
now go on back there and behave yourself or we'll have to put you
in the zoo with the other animals
that's when that old lady remembers coils torso arms her hands
touches echo hollow sorrow
howls the day
hears the wind the air the water odors warm of sun
the cool of the trees
the real of the round brown ground
the bugs the birds the animals
remembers feels the love their faces
the gifts from the grandmothers and grandfathers
her mommys daddys grannys grampas auntys uncles cousins
thighs hips arms
their faces
their faces who heal
their faces
who give her life
right at the level of life

III

this is around the time the folks in whitetown
invite the old lady to speak about her metis ancestors
down at the writer's retreat
she tells them she's seen family friends elders babes
murdered and mutilated
seen ravenblack brown braids hanging from a white picket fence
different sizes textures thickness styles
and no one speaks to her after that
three days of silence and then
vegetarian breakfast in bed
served by one of her teachers from the senior high
the one who teaches the old lady how to make a mug
whispers it's so wonderful that you have so much love to give
after all you've been through
no eye contact
that teacher pulls out inspects her mechanical pencil
removes the eraser
puts back the eraser
removes it
lifts her eyes looks
looks down at the old lady
whispers you have to break them in slowly
smiles you have to break them in gently
I am many things says the old lady
happy and beautiful with braided hair
is what the auntys say
taking all that dreamtime and giving so much back
lights a fire at first light
lights a fire and thanks our creator
for this new day
this new life
right at the level of life

Mr. Season

The cottage smells musty, even though we arrived four days ago. Like all Indian summer days at the cottage, it has been long and full of excitement. My seven year old sister, Kim, is jumping on my stomach. She yells, "It's time! Get dressed, or you're going to miss Mr. Season!"

In a blurred state, I put my feet on the cold, dusty floor and stand to put on my fourth-time-hand-me-down shorts. Kim grabs a white t-shirt, rips off my pyjama top, and prepares to thrust the clean garment over my head.

"Hands up!" she yells.

Then she is running out the door and I am yelling after her, "wait for me . . . ple-e-e-ease!"

Southward we run, toward West Lake. It is a small but famous lake attached to Lake Ontario in Prince Edward County, just outside of the town of Wellington. My Great Aunt and Uncle, Betty and Hank Young, own three cottages next to their house. The great yard in between their home and the cottages is sectioned off. There are two horseshoe pits, each with four horseshoes. Next is a field where us kids used to dance in, play frisbee and baseball. The waterfront is next, with a skinny beach and a long dock at the southernmost end of the property.

We are headed to the dock, as Mr. Season only comes out at this time in the morning. Kim and I sneak slowly to the end of the dock and dangle our dirty feet over the edge. We quietly wait.

"Sssshhhhh," she says.

It seems like hours pass by. I notice a crab crawling toward the dock near the beach, but I dare not visit him—Mr. Season is surely expecting our attendance this morning. Suddenly the dock shakes, and Kim and I, startled, look at each other and then toward the beach.

"Oh," she says with a sigh of relief. "Its only those two." It is my brothers trying to sneak up on us. Craig is eleven, and Brett is nine. "Okay you guys, you can stay today, but only if you are quiet and polite. Mr. Season doesn't like surprises."

And just as Craig and Brett try to squeeze onto the end of the dock with my sister and me, he comes. Quietly at first, he swims by and pretends not to notice us—I think he is shy today. Soon enough though, he comes over to share some knowledge with us. Unfortunately, we don't speak his language anymore, so I can't ask him how old he is.

Mr. Season floats there—I know he is studying us as we study him. Surely he does so with the same amazement. As we look closer, we can see four wondrous colours in his shell. On the right side, there are yellow streaks like the morning sun. The end near his tail is as dark as the night—also as dark as it gets in our house when Dad is mad at Mom and she makes us go into the bedroom without any lights on. His left side has beautiful clay-red streaks which stand out next to the white spots near his head. It looks as if he has been sprinkled with the most delicate snow.

Then Brett starts to get a bloody nose—this often happens when he gets excited—and he jerks his arm to catch the crimson-coloured blood. Too much! He has scared Mr. Season, who surges under the surface into the depths of the lake.

"Thanks a lot, Brett," the three of us shout.

"He'll never come back again," I say. I run away towards the house, followed by Kim, and Craig starts to skip rocks on the water as Brett stands alone on the dock.

My sister and I run back to the cottage. Kim asks Mom where Dad is and she replies, "he's drinking with your Uncle, as usual."

Kim says, "But Mom, Sarah Jane told me that her mother told her that people just don't drink before noon."

"Well, your father is on vacation and he feels he can do whatever he wants."

"So does that mean that we can do whatever we want?" I ask.

"Well, you can do whatever you want as long as you don't hurt yourselves, you stay on the property and out of the water, and you are back by noon—that's two hours from now." No sooner have the words come out of her mouth than we shoot out the door like a speeding train.

And so the morning passes with our explorations but all too soon, Mom is calling us in to the lunch she has prepared. Dad doesn't show up for the meal, so she saves him the best vegetables, cold meats and the biggest bun. When he's with Uncle Hank, we never know when he'll show up. And he always shows up hungry.

After lunch, Craig and Brett leave to go play "boy games" while Kim and I help with the dishes. You see, that's the way we have been raised—the girls clean the house and sometimes the yard, and the men and boys of the house can generally do as they please.

Afterwards, we all split up again to enjoy the woundrous, soothing and warming rays of sunshine on our backs. The day slips by and soon it is supper time. Kim and I always knew what we were having for the meal long before the boys did, because Mom never let them in the cottage while we were preparing the food. The cottage was too small, and the boys always got in the way. Tonight, we have a wonderful feast of cooked ham, hash-brown casserole (and oh how wonderful that is!), fresh biscuits and fresh corn.

Four o'clock. Supper is almost ready, and Kim places the plates neatly on the table while I carefully put the silverware in its proper position. Just the way Dad likes it. Mom does the biscuits last, as Dad is very particular about them—they have to be warm still, and buttered just-the-right-amount. One hour passes.

It is now five o'clock, and the five us are uneasily sitting in place, our little tummies rumbling. I ask if we can go ahead without Dad, and my sister hits me.

"I'll tell you what," Mom says, "you go play, and if he isn't here by six, then we'll start without him."

Six o'clock comes, and six o'clock goes. I start to feel sick, and finally she lets us begin the feast around six thirty.

It doesn't take long before we are all full, yet not satisfied. We feel very uneasy. My eldest brother, Craig, asks if we can be excused, but Mom tells us to stay longer just in case Dad shows up soon.

"You know how he insists on the family being together for supper," she says. So we wait. And we wait.

Soon we hear laughing voices coming towards the cottage.

"Bye, Lloyd! Tell that beautiful family of yours that I'll see them tomorrow!" Uncle Hank says.

Dad arrives. He sees that we have eaten and is unhappy, but says nothing to us as he sits down and demands his warm biscuits, buttered just-the-right way. Mom tells him that they are cold now, because he is very late.

He yells, "You better have those god-damned buns warmed and on the table now, or else." Or else. That was a common saying of his. I ask Mom if we (the children) can go to our room now.

She says yes, but Dad bellows, "No. You are going to sit here and you are going to do it until I am done eating. That's what a good family does. But I guess you wouldn't know about that."

So we sit and we shudder. Mom tries hard to please him, but he wants the biscuits too soon. He yells at her, saying they are not warm enough. She tries to explain that he'll have to eat them the way they are. That's it. Not the right thing to say.

He stands up and shakes the table, and one-by-one, throws our four empty plates to the floor. One-by-one, they crash and break into little pieces; a myriad of colour, just like Mr. Season's back.

Mom sends us to our room. We run with our arms around each other, united in fear. We sit on the edge of the bed, hugging, shivering, crying. I am sitting somewhere in the middle. We hear everything going on, especially since only a thin, old orange blanket-doubled-as-a-door separates us from them.

I know this has happened before, only I don't remember. I am scared of my father, but I don't know why. We hear him pushing Mom around. She repeatedly asks him to stop because he is scaring "the children." From our room comes muffled, tear-choked pleas of "please stop, Daddy, we'll be good." He takes her into their bedroom and continues to scream and throw things around.

Suddenly, I snap. I don't realize it at the time, but I forget how big and scary Dad is to me. I jump off the bed, and as I run to the door, Craig tries to grab me. "Don't go out there!" he shouts as I leave the room. Adrenaline pumping through every inch of my body, I enter my parent's room just in time to see my Dad raise his hand in the air. I continue my motion and use every fibre of my being to move towards him. Instinct has its way with me. It throws me into my mother's lap with my back to her. I face my father with my finger in his face, and I yell with all my might, "Don't you dare lay a hand on my mother, or else!"

In an instant his hand is raised again, only to me this time. His face is full of rage. I close my eyes, realizing suddenly that he is far too powerful for me. I cringe. I can hear my older brothers and sister whining and whimpering in their room. All is silent. My mom's arms surround me tightly, in the only protection-hold she knows. Silence comes from my father. Silence, anger, tension, greed. The smell of rye is seeping from every crevice of his body. He raises his hand higher. Then slowly, he drops it. And he leaves.

I hug Mom and tell her everything will be alright.

In seconds, my brothers and sister all surround Mom. Happy we have survived this one. Hoping he won't come back until tomorrow, when he is sober. And he doesn't.

I sleep with my Mom. Soon I am dreaming of Mr. Season and his many wonderful colours. Only this time; only this night, the darkness from the end of his shell is gone. Tonight, his yellows, reds and whites stand out in a glowing splendour. And he smiles at me. And everything is alright.

For tonight.

The Healing
(Dedicated to my Sister and Brother)

I try to dance
I cannot
My Nishnawbe body
My Nishnawbe spirit
will not move, but have abandoned me.
I am empty, alone
and suffer in silence
I have forgotten who I am
Where I come from
Remember, try to remember
but I am weak and close my eyes,
I dream.
Visions of Ancestors
Dancing, in circles
My mother dances, my father dances
Ribbons of red, black, yellow and white
swirl around the fire
I hear drums
and see Eagles fly
I smell the sacred odours
I am bathed in smoke
and feel strength and power of many Ancestors
dancing, singing out
Not just for me
But for all
Who need their healing
My mother smiles, my father nods
"You are *Nishnawbe* blood"
"You are strong"
"You are Indian"
"This song we sing from the spirit world and you are not ready to join us"
"Your life shall continue its full journey, gathering wisdom for your spirit"
"And strength for your body"
"And you will dance again."
"We'll all dance again."
Meegwetch.

MIXED BLOODS

Mountains stand, towering and ageless
strong rock faces pressed together in immutable solidity
families and tribes all one.

Rain and heat and cold beat down over the ages
weathering only the surface.
Never the bones.

Come the invaders with their dynamite, their rifle fire
shattering rock.
Creating cracks and separating shards to send them flying
far from the mother rock.

They lie alone, lost in the streams of detritus
washing down from everywhere.
Forgetting where they came from.

Worn to grains of sand,
and finally to dirt,
they merge helplessly with other

Until they seem like other,
look like other,
are thought to be other
indistinguishable in lost sameness.

But they are still shards of the mother rock,
needing to go home
to help build the mountain again.

BIOGRAPHY OF A PERSON OF SUBSTANCE

I saw her twice a week for months at a time, until she stopped coming for awhile. Then, a few months later, she'd start coming again. The rules were set early, by her. She would only come when she could pay me the agreed-upon fee, and she'd make do when she couldn't. If things got too bad, she could call me, but she would not call unless she knew she wouldn't make it through the night. Those were the rules.

When she first started coming, she wore the same clothes every time. Washed almost bare of color, her jeans and sweatshirt under-pinned by worn, washed tennis shoes were always, always clean. Once she told me she had a lot of other clothes, but she only wore that outfit, as she felt like people stared at her and laughed at her if she wore anything else. These clothes made her almost invisible. She wasn't so afraid when she wore them.

She didn't go out where people could see her if she could avoid it. People were always staring at her, and whispering, and laughing at her. Yeah, she worked, but people always laughed at her there, too. They all knew, somehow. They knew about what had happened at her last job. It was that time she sneezed. Oh, God. They knew. Everybody knew. That's why she only went to get groceries at 2:00 a.m. in the morning, because it was a small town, and everybody knew. Her boyfriend protected her, and took her to the store then, so nobody could see her, even in her clean, worn sweatshirt and jeans.

She liked to come for therapy, though. She liked the smell of cedar and sage, and the wolf pictures on the wall. She loved talk-ing, cuddled and comforted by the books entirely surrounding us, keeping us safe. In summer, she was happy, talking outside in the little lathe house, with all the pots of madly blooming fuschias moving gently in the breeze, and Moonbeam stretched out in catly splendor just at the corner of her vision, soaking up sunrays. It made it easier to tell me what had happened.

Even in winter, with frozen rain or snow outside, she liked it there in the office, warm and snug with books and guardian wolves.

It was just so hard. There were so many people who didn't

understand. People who laughed. People who knew. People who sneered, or would if they knew. If they could see her in spite of the magic sweatshirt, jeans, and worn tennis shoes.

Well, yes, if she remembered correctly, things weren't always so great when she was little, either. Her father drank, you know. He got mean when he was drunk. Smashed 'em all around just for the hell of it. Mom ended up in the hospital a lot. She could see why her brothers all beat on her, and made her do things. Not their fault, what with Daddy like that. But she knew she could fix them, if they'd just listen to reason. Maybe she'd go on back home, talk some sense into Mom and Daddy. Maybe next summer.

I enjoyed seeing her. She was so polite, so proud, and so damn likable. I'd call her when she hadn't come to see me for a couple of months. Truth was, I missed her, and worried about her. But, no, she wouldn't come in unless she could pay me. Those were the rules. It'd get pretty bad, sometimes. The FBI knew now. Her phone was tapped, and her landlady had been in her house, stole some letters and notes. They were really on her ass at work. Laughing at her behind her back, said she was crazy because she was seeing me. OK. She'd go in to see the doctor and get some medications. OK. She'd come and see me; she'd find the money. She liked it there in the office. It smelled so good. We were both glad to see each other.

It was a glorious late summer day, and the fuschias were vying for attention in their swinging baskets. A rare hot afternoon, not a cloud in the turquoise sky. On time as usual, her turquoise blouse was the exact color of the sky, and her running shoes were so white they hurt my eyes. Her beautiful dark eyes sparkled as she told me all about her trip to the grocery store yesterday afternoon. Stuff looks different in daylight!

The Community Is Starving

The jeep and the truck were coming down the road in different directions. Snow piled the side of the road and it snowed again. An animal appeared to have jumped on the road, looked like a wolf. Professor Windale turned to miss the animal and crash! He hit Carleen's truck. Impact. And his jeep went into a snow bank. He banged his head on the steering wheel. After the impact, Carleen and Eric got out of the truck. Professor Windale was unconscious. They went to check him.

It was a long harsh winter on this west coast. Game was scarce. The community, a small Longhouse with five families, was starving. Two hunters went hunting one last time. In the woods, they came upon a clearing. A semi-circle of wolves were there with two deer in the centre. The two hunters stepped forward for the deer. They were grateful. The hunters returned home with the deer. Weary as they were they made it. It was for the survival of the family. Aaron Windale saw his community. The family in the longhouse was asking, *"Are you our hunter?"*

The smell of ocean salt the taste of wind, set. Aaron was in the Longhouse with the family. The young and old were drained of energy. Starving, they were. He could see it on their faces and their frames were thin. Where were their hunters? The community turned to Aaron asking, "Are you our hunter?"

"Can I be their hunter?"

"No! No!"

Close to the university, they were fifteen minutes outside of the city. Carleen held Professor Windale as he sweated and thrashed about. Then he moved to consciousness.

"Are you alright, Professor?"

"Ah." He looked beside him and recognized students from the university.

"Carleen and Eric isn't it? What are you two doing here?"

"Our vehicles hit, sir, and you went unconscious."

"I remember now. I was working, marking papers at the university and I was making my way home. It snowed. Always snows deep in November. Did you see that wolf? I turned to miss it and we hit."

Carleen looked at Eric and he shrugged his shoulder. She responded, "What wolf? I didn't see any wolf. But we did hit. I was worried when you didn't wake."

"I cannot believe where I was."

"You were right here, Professor."

"Ah ... oh ya right. How long was I out?"

"About a minute," answered Eric.

A minute after one o'clock and he had ten more assignments to mark. God, did he feel sorry for some of his students. He saw their inability to grasp the easiest of concepts and use them to complete the task at hand. If they had just did it they way he outlined, they would be fine. Fine.

Will anything ever be fine again?

Professor Windale sat in the driver's seat and Carleen and Eric stood by the window, in the snow.

"How are our vehicles?"

"Dents. But, your jeep and my truck are pretty tough,"replied Carleen.

"What have you two been doing since English last year?"

Carleen looked at Eric then answered, "We are both taking courses. Today we were going to the campus library to study calculus and edit poetry."

"You're still writing, then? There's usually a few you hope will continue their literary pursuits."

"Oh, yes. I still write."

No one spoke for moments. Carleen and Eric began feeling the cold. Professor Windale sat back. And he did go there.

Again he stirred.

"Professor. Sir, you went unconscious again. We'll take you to the hospital. We'll be there in about twenty minutes. I'll drive you. And Eric, will you drive my truck?

"No mistaking it this time, my family called me."

Carleen and Eric looked at each other and shrugged. Carleen said "Shall we go Professor?"

Professor Windale slowly moved over to the passenger seat. Carleen looked at Eric.

"Sure Carleen, I'll drive your truck."

She smiled and gave him her keys. Carleen climbed into

Professor Windale's jeep. She geared up, looked at Professor Windale before she drove away. No blowing snow hindered her sight. It had stopped snowing now, though it was getting dark this late winter afternoon.

"I signed up for a Poetry Workshop, Fiction Workshop, Art Theory and of course calculus as a math elective. That's why Eric and I have been studying together. Our studies and career goals are worlds away but I needed help with Calculus. In return, I workshop his poetry assignments with him. Numbers are his focus. Words are mine."

His head was pulsing his headache. "Oh ... I have no focus at all this moment."

"You know, it was a cousin of mine who suggested this university. Nowadays, when she's not working, she spends a lot of time on the powwow circuit because her children dance. We have a nice elementary and high school program on our reserve and my grades were high. Rosey was my first relative to go onto university. Did you grow up on a reservation, Professor Windale?"

"Carleen, you can call me Aaron." He paused momentarily then continued, "I have not thought about my community until tonight. I never knew my parents and I have never been to see my community. So, no I never grew up on the reserve."

Carleen drove the jeep. Her truck followed close behind. Aaron sat next to her. Fidgeting, he moved uncomfortably in his seat. In silence they drove. Thoughts of his people emerged after all these years.

"So, how are your classes doing, Aaron?"

"Surviving."

"You or your students?" She laughed.

"Was I really that bad?"

"Well, I learned very much from your class."

"I lay it out right from the beginning that we do this then this and we learn ..."

"I know. I know. I always wondered how much room we had for interpretation."

"Interpretation. I introduce the class to a process, logical and practical, what they do with it is their choice."

"What is still suspect, though, is where does this process come from?"

"Suspect? Sounds like you're saying my upbringing and lessons from society and university are invalid."

"Not invalid. But it is important to think about where you come from and the culture."

"I do not feel like agreeing or disagreeing with what you are saying. Something happened to me after our accident."

"Oh?"

Aaron sat forward putting hands to his head and spoke, "I visited my community or most likely my community visited me. This was about two hundred years or more and the community was starving. Their bodies were so thin and god did they need help. They asked me to be their hunter."

"And...."

He banged his left hand with his other fist.

"Damn it! I don't even have a gun! No gun! How can I be their hunter when I am not prepared?"

Tears. Aaron cried. Carleen looked to him. They drove in silence for a couple of minutes.

"Wow, that was a powerful vision. I don't know if this will help but my grandpa told me to strive to provide for people. And Aaron, something to think about is that providing for the community in the 1990s is different than hundreds of years ago."

Carleen pulled into the hospital parking lot. His tears were spent. Aaron was thinking about his reserve and how to begin contributing to his community.

"Maybe. I know one place I can start is my community's school. I can send boxes of books for their library and I'll send my resume to the administration there."

He turned to Carleen and said, "thank you for driving me. I appreciate you being there and for your words."

Carleen smiled. Aaron walked into the hospital.

The Burning

When you get home take a shower and hang out your clothes in case the spirits forget something. I shivered and looked at the ocean. Forget something? What would a spirit forget, and whatever it is, what would it be doing on my clothes?

Auntie Irene was quietly sitting in her chair observing the activities of the burning. Our ancestors are ingenious; a burning is the cleansing of the soul, a release of the deep and unreachable grief. I glanced at the bag of wool I was offering to my Grandma through the fire.

Would the wool be enough? Would she be pleased? Although I was only twelve when my Grandma died, memories of her stayed with me like they were glued to my brain. Grandma had a strong presence. She was a force of fire herself. She survived many hardships, including a brother who was killed in a residential school. He was strung up and beaten for punching a vice-principal. This is what I have been told by a stranger, who later told about it on television. My family has never mentioned it.

I try to focus on the happy memories. Like the times Grandma cut fish and hung them up in the shed to be smoked. All of those pieces of reddish brown fish, hanging downward from the beams were an awesome sight. I can think of no other words to describe the image. Sometimes Grandma would give lessons to my cousins and me, usually on how to shuck shellfish or how to fry bread. She had a daring, almost impish, smile when she cracked open oysters and swallowed them whole. The grey mass of flesh was repulsive, and I was impressed.

The happy memories are wishy-washy without any clear borders. They disappear quickly when I see the anger on her face. As a young child, it seemed to me Grandma was angry a lot. Never marry a white man, she would say to me. It will never work. At the age of eight I tried to let on that I understood. Grandma, I believe, was disappointed that I, and my sisters and brother were half white. Correction, we are Indians with white ancestors too.

I think she forgave my father, her oldest son. Still, this did not take away from her disappointment. I could feel the anger, the heat within her. She was angry, I assume, at the world. I did not understand then where that anger came from. Why it builds and engulfs. I believe I understand now.

With my back to the fire, I ask Grandma to guide me. I want to make peace. We are all standing with our backs to the fire so the spirits can eat their food offerings in privacy. The wind is strong. My hands are turning red. The wind carries our ancestors to the fire on the beach where we are gathered to feed them, to pay tribute to their needs in the spirit world. The wind is them.

I try not to glance around at the others as the spirits feast. It is not proper to observe someone's grief. Grief is a private thing. Standing still is hard. My attention wanders after I feel satisfied with my silent conversations with Grandma and my friend Colleen.

For Colleen, I bring offerings of cigarettes. These are placed on a food plate and burned. I feel a little guilty, for I only bring half a pack. I think to myself that Colleen would not mind, and she would be happy to share with me. She was a good friend from childhood and was until she was killed by a drunken driver at the age of twenty.

Colleen was beautiful. She had curly dark hair, sparkling eyes, and a mischievous smile. She would often tease me, knowing that I was easy to tease.

She would plan chances to tease me. We spent hours together doing young girl things, and later the business of teenagers. We walked to the store, played on the beach and experimented with make-up. She was the make-up applier and I was the excited student. To be transformed was exciting to me then. I guess I believed the make-up went deeper than my skin. Sometimes, in summer days, Colleen and I pretended wonderful adventures like we were trapped walking in a desert.

She also told me she loved me. This is the first memory I have of anyone ever saying that to me. I could not say it back. The feeling was there, but got stuck inside. I could not make myself vulnerable. By this time, I knew without articulating my theories or thoughts, about being vulnerable. At fourteen or fifteen, I was tightly bound. Impenetrable, or so I thought and wished.

My first real lesson in the damaging of innocence occurred

with Colleen's death. The offender received a few months in a prison work camp and his driver's license was taken away for a year. A few months, a year, for a beautiful being. For years afterward, her sparkling eyes would turn red with blood in my sleep.

After her death there were whispers around our town of; "What were they doing out that late at night?" My sister was with her and witnessed her death. Colleen and my sister were judged and found at fault. "Drunken Indians" was the sentiment implied. "Why didn't they hear the car?" I was shocked and hurt. My innocent self would thereafter have a big hole.

I am pleased with my offering to Colleen. I know she is happy with the cigarettes. I know, just as the people standing around the fire know, that the Eagles flying over are showing us their approval. The spirits are also the Eagles.

As we get ready to leave the fire, I hope that the cedar branch tucked into my purse is large enough to protect me. It is a pretty small piece. A woman, a person I do not know, brushes the branch over my body and asks the spirits to guide me and to keep me healthy. I silently thank her.

I do not know enough about these activities. I know my ancestors do not want to hurt me. But, I am afraid. I shower and hang out my clothes on my patio. I live in a modern condo. It is a large pinkish building stuck in the middle of trees. It is a new development or what many of us feel, new damage to the Valley.

I live here because for the moment it is the closest I can get to home. Home is at the bottom of the hill by the water.

At night I fear the spirits may come to my clothes, forgetting something and perhaps, come into my apartment. I pull the covers closer to my body, and hope that I remembered to shut the windows tightly. I am exhausted. I had to take a nap earlier when I left the burning. Grieving is hard work.

Before falling asleep, I chide myself for my ignorance and my fear. As a young girl I did not know I was an "Indian." I use the word Indian off-handedly, and sometimes cringe. The proper political term is Aboriginal or First Nations person. I want to be proper.

As a young girl, I didn't see the difference in the colour of my father's skin from my own. My sisters, brother and I are dark-haired with fair, freckled skin. My mother is very fair, blonde and blue-eyed. She is descended from a Scottish family. My father is brown.

"You are an Indian, and you should be proud," is what my father explained to me when I was six or seven years old. "Never forget that." When I think of it, I feel gratitude for this gift from my father, this anchor that he knew I would need in later life. At the same time, he would make affectionate jokes about my freckles. I was ashamed of my freckles, until my Scottish family told me they were a sign of beauty. I wanted to believe them.

Approaching mid-life, I look at my younger self and feel sad. I grieve for myself and for my losses. I was eight when I came to realize that there was something special about me. There was something special about who I was and where I came from. I smile now, remembering when I learned about my specialness, I tried to rain dance. A rain dance is not part of my family's culture, and was never spoken about, but it was the only thing that came to my mind about Indians.

I walked around a driveway with an old apple tree branch and chanted something. I prayed hard for it to rain. I was very disappointed when it did not. It was a scorching hot day in August. I walked back to my home with my head down.

I feel both disgust and compassion for my younger self. Disgust because of my vulnerability and compassion, because I tried to embrace myself without knowing how. I still try to embrace myself without really knowing how. I continue to try, and hope that my sincerity for the values of my ancestors will make up for my ignorance.

The burning is a soul cleansing. Perhaps next time I should bring an offering for what haunts me from the past. Burn my make-up to remove past shames of my looks? Burn some of my books to remove shame of my ignorance? I need something that will represent my whole life, but I cannot think of what.

I can blame no one person. My Grandma lived in a world, of what seemed to me to be, of hate. Children were taught by people who were supposed to be religious, to unlearn who they were, and to be ashamed of themselves. The instructions were veiled with concern on the one hand, and with violence, usually on the other.

I have learned that violence is just not physical force. Violence is also the deadly self-righteousness of one person or group believing they have a right to rob others of their spirit by whatever means. Someone tried to rob Grandma's spirit. While damage was done, I really don't know if they were successful.

I know so little of my past. My father did not learn to teach me. In his younger days our hill was referred to as the dirty Indian hill. The phrase was "Siwash Hill." Even now my father spends a lot of time cleaning, pressing, and perfecting his clothes. He removes all of the creases, even in his blue jeans. He works to remove the possibility of anyone whispering that he belongs to Siwash Hill.

In the last moments of waking, I decide that I am safe. If a spirit does enter my place, it will enter for good purposes and not bad ones. I reflect on Auntie Irene rising from her chair; the contrast of her aging body and her powerful presence. I think about her wisdom in holding this gathering. I wonder if I will be able to teach my grandchildren about a burning.

Joanne Peter

Look Within And Accept

At this precise second.
I am up to my eyebrows in resentments, grudges
and mistakes.
They are clouding over my eyes.
The windows to my spirit.

I want to run to a distant hillside.
And talk to the Great Spirit.
I will find the answers within me and all around
me.

Then I will accept myself as I am.
And the wind will slowly take my troubles away.
As I face up to them one by one.

(Written February 10, 1982)

"Digehwi"
(Blind)

The long path chosen
Is an honourable one for me.
I walk in a tight circle,
What is given always returning.

I am not alone on this path,
Grandmother is here to watch,
Grandfathers are here to protect.
Family. Here to give strength.

Others gaze with bewilderment,
Not comprehending the respect,
Unaware of what is around them.
I gaze back with equal confusion.
How can one not see the circle,
The respect which breeds honour?
Can they, will they ever see?
I walk in a tight circle.

A Healing Stone

I miss that stone
The one that Bette gave me
It was shaped like a heart
That's why I chose it
because mine was broken
I held it sometimes when memory chills from past
would come to toy with my soul
There was something
about holding that stone
from the Mediterranean Sea
Bette said that's where it came from
She mused that Jesus walked on it
There was comfort emanating from that stone
and many people touched it
as I shared the story of pain
that brought it to me
Maybe that's why I've lost the stone
because my heart has healed
So, if you ever find a stone
shaped like a heart
Remember to hold it close
It was touched by many people
And it has the power to heal

Beyond

The Theology of Turbulence
Lenny Peoples, Indian Village Tour Guide and
unofficial tribal historian, slaughters sacred cows.

Myth Number One: Indians are lazy and untaxed.
This is what they tell the masses,
here we dine on bread and roses.
While you suffer, punch time cards,
we fancy dance and don't pay taxes.

**Myth Number Two: Any successful Indian must be supported
by Communists, Republicans or Organized Crime.**
Cherokee to the bone.
(we forgive the Powhatan)
Wayne's a self-made man.
Beanbread gave him that double chin,
hominy, grits and black-eyed peas.
Wayne Newton's no gangster, we'd bet the casino.
Mobsters prefer red sauce and pasta.

Myth Number Three: Indians are natural scouts.
Here is the truth, I don't care how they tell it:
Columbus was dumb as a box of rocks,
and lost to boot, which makes it worse.
Once a year, we stay home, treat conquistador-free nations
for a chance to surpass us, get ahead for a day.
All courtesy of a man so foolish,
he really believed you couldn't fall off the world.
Big hands, swelled feet, the smell of onions,
Boy so country he sailed for Spain.
Where the queen was inbred and never took a bath.
Every time he whispered the name of God,
it was more for the sake of his soul than ours.

Myth Number Four: All Indians drive broken-down "Rez Cars."
Rez Car?
Thirty miles an hour.
We'd make grand entry faster walking.

But my wife longs to jingle dance,
so we drive all night in straight lines and circles.
Rez car?
Roof leaks cold stormwater.
We stay warm on the idea of dry.
But my wife craves drums,
so we stay late and sleep in the seats.

We make our own thunder.

Myth Number Five: Indians are childlike and honest.
I'd say we're truthful to a fault,
telling the Pilgrims they could stay.
No one owned the earth, anyway.
It grew squash, regardless of colour.
We told them our numbers and our ways.
Our hearts were such glass, they were broken by smallpox.

But one lie we told, and we're not a bit sorry.
We started the rumour that the world was flat.
Came by night to trouble the Vikings,
shook them sober with rattle and bone,
made their Greenland disappear,
sent survivors home with the fear
that maybe you could sail over the edge.
Stay home, we whispered, don't tempt Leviathan.
We had peace and quiet for quite a few years.

Myth Number Six: Indians make loyal sidekicks for cowboys, anthropologists and lonely rangers.
Tonto knew it first and best:
syndication means much wampum.

Myth Number Seven: Most White Americans have a great-great grandmother, who happened to be a Cherokee princess.
First things first, we've no such thing.
If you'd said Beloved Woman, I might have bought it.
As for red women, even though you've no crown,

think twice before taking their rings for your blankets.
Remember the rift between whiskey and water.
Whiskey makes mistakes, talks to strangers.
Clean water keeps its distance.
Why would you brave the adventure of whiskey.
Swallow snake-handling,
truth or dare?
Stay home, choose us, let them find other queens.

Myth Number Eight: Indians, by rubbing two sticks together, can start fires and survive in the woods.
Always
carry a road atlas
trade your flint for Zippo lighters
trust only your father's compass
Abstain from everything
but love.

Myth Number Nine: Indians have no natural fear of heights.
In the air,
I am lost.
I misplace hope
without my feet.
In the air,
I am lost.
No room for my soul when I have wings.

Myth Number Ten: All Indians are excellent horsemen.
Some trust in horses.
I trust in dance.
I am a bad son of a gun,
fearless of flying,
spinning,
leaping
into the powwow sky.
When I dance,
I high-five God.

Red

In his new poem
the red autumn woods
are a metaphor
for leftist martyrs
We are travelling east through a maple forest
that blazes the hillsides on both sides of this winding
back-country road Look at the trees I want to tell him
Listen The trees have their own stories to tell
like the story of fire deep within the heart They too
have been martyrs in the long war against the land, a nation
cut down, children denied
A hundred years ago these hills were bare of trees
the stone walls that wind through them
the illusion of ownership Now the hills are red with maples
My heart is leaping out to meet them, my eyes
can not be full enough Though acid falls from the clouds
maples have gathered on the hillsides
in every direction See how they celebrate
They are wearing their brightest dresses
Come sisters, let me dance with you
I offer you a song
Let me paint
it red with
passion
You are
all the women
I have ever loved

Trees

Trees are the greatest witnesses of all,
they are all truth, good and bad.

It is with truth they utter their stories to us.
They peer in our houses, made of wood.

They recoil at our shrieking, screaming and rumbling.
I am wood,
A tree helped make me.
My arms are branches,
and my legs are a hard wood, with marbled markings.

Trees, like us, are bound to earth
without hope of liberation, save death.

Do they feel? Do they see, have they senses?
A phenomenal amount more than we.

They house us, we murder them,
They heal us, we murder them,
They shade us, we murder them.

They have no means of suicide,
their fate is in our hands.

Their nations don't fight, and yet we
attack the armless totems and throw
seeds and sapling as their defence.

A tree has a voice, whether I'm there to hear it or not.
Speak to us trees and alert us to what you see coming
from your vantage points.
Reach high in the sky,
and offer your arms for the winged to rest,
for they too are messengers to us.

The first time I understood the trees.
they told me there is no greater artist,
than Mother Earth.
We need to get back to our roots.
Long life to you trees, thank you.

All things

Knowledge is power,
Sex is power,
Faith is power,
Unity is power,
Money is power,
Nature is power,
Simplicity is power,
Animals are power,
Truth is power,
Wisdom is power,
Balance is power,
Talent is power,
Courage is power,
Fear is power,
Beauty is power
Music is power,
Silence is power,
Love is power,
I am power,
You are power,
We are power,
Imagination is power,
Peace is power
Words are power,
Repetition is power.

BEINGNESS SONG

I play with the words like a fox
With a bone from the pile on the altar
Of souls losing lives in some
Ritualized gift of victims to gods
Who might want them
For glory in each others' eyes.

The words have been kidnapped
and battered and bedded,
notched and disfigured, twisted off
senses that skip on the mainstream
like canning jar lids and cheap
brand name wrappers torn off to make
labels for word-codes like 'dance,'
'spirit,' 'vision,' 'dream,' 'song,'
'my relations,' and more bits of lizard tails
posing as lizards in minds that see tokens
and sources as solidly same.

The words may have flown or been stolen:
The thoughts they were born from have always been Home.
I celebrate.   (I am)
I honour.
I celebrate.   (I act)
I honour.
I celebrate.   (I live)
I am honoured.

MAKING DO

Grandfather, if a Blackfoot Warrior returned for a time as a bear,
        would he still be a Blackfoot Warrior?
Grandmother, if a Cree life-giver returned for a time as a fox,
        would she still be a Cree life-giver?

You teach me to welcome the ancestors when they return
        as our neighbour's children,
        as we will someday be welcomed,
        as we will someday return.

Grandmother, when the white man came we were many,
100 million they say.
In a few centennials, only 10 of those millions remain.
So. Now I have 90 million ancestors.
Do you think they have waited all this time?
Do you think they just sit still and wait?

Grandmother, should I believe the pale-eyed lawyer who stands in the
        courts on the side of Aboriginal Rights?
Grandfather, if a Blackfoot Warrior returned for a time as a pale-eyed
        lawyer, would he still be a Blackfoot Warrior?

(Ma-kwah, I knows you. I ride your Bear's neck to beyond.
Kokum of Bear Clan, your claws mark the door to my home.
Old Ones, you could run many pale bodies, change many minds.
Welcome. Their priests grant them only one life for all time.
Well. Come. We have much to do. We'll make do.)

about love connections

our self sustained
imprimaturs
acknowledge our
tenuous toeholds on
spiritual science

clown alley still serves
great hamburgers on lombard
street in san francisco
and the spatenhaus in
downtown munich serves the
best wienerschnitzel
on the planet

good memories build layers of
recognition to trade in
for rubber stamp lifetimes

synthetic variables force us
to understand the commonplace
as well as the exceptional
kinda like looking for a
cancer gene in every bowl
of soup ever served

small pox blankets were
never ruled unethical-in fact
were commended by most
authorities over time as
logical cleansers for
savage removal

but the son of mystery
walked among the folk
in that old world

and his main job was
to be the love connection

sex and puritans are so boring
so off the wall and party line at the
same time.

who cares if genders
can't figure the real mystery
is somewhere between bodies
and yet nowhere
buried deep
in mother earth

he came to be the
love connection
he came to authorize
duplicates of himself
NOT temples filled
with memorabilia
to be run by
self appointed big daddies

Untitled

images shift internally
crowd bananas and marmalade
out of existence
wish i could divide and conquer
all my own bad habits as
prelude to shooting down
the moon in someone
else's lovestruck psyche

i am overwhelmed with neglect
not knowing where to begin
my reclamation and restoration
of all appropriate behaviours—
those moods required of civilized beings

others seek treasured value
in order to tranquillize all
foreign substances—
any out of hand stray cat idea
or exciting misadventure

why can't i see simple solutions
and april stormy nights
in ample quantities when
i need to
knowing the balm of attainment
will soften the corners of my
harsh observations and smooth
unwarranted judgements into
harmless opinions with a
negative twist.

Mountain drops

The illusion is dreamscaping
once a year
we often
second guess the spell
tantalizing colours
    burst from
      the mountain side
send a message
scanning,
picking up sound
millions of honey bees
    swarm
      the crisp air
wild violets pop the soil
that only weeks ago
layered
    a cool bed
      on a frost blanket
down at the creekside
cubs snipe
at fresh mineral water
burst an explosion of minnows
    savoured by land animals
      existence
birdsong humming the ear
over miles of mosaic
painted hills splashed with colour
sweeping the message from
    one end of the valley
      to another.
I shivered
the spell had arrived
and would soon disappear
    with the first orange sunset
      on a hot dusk evening

It was only ...Yesterday

A child plays ecstatically in the midst of the floor,
It may seem distracting to the eyes of the beholder, but,
Love me as I truly am a gift to you,
Until death shall we be departed.

A teen draws a picture of compassion and remorse,
Feelings of inferior and complexities, surely,
Needing a compelling place in your heart,
Growing maturely with a tender smile.

If a teardrop has forgiven me,
Emotionally drained from all the grieving, somehow,
There is a compassionate heart in others,
The nature of my personal tribute in life.

I have grown maturely in solitude,
Every moment, every second counts, somewhere,
For the love I have shared with one and all,
Grateful to be alive for another day.

Stephen Andrews

He learned shorthand between two careers,
a man whose life was defined by his work,
not his family.

Who was she, the woman who opened his doors
to find Texan spit in her face for what her husband
believed in?

Was his shorthand the way to her children,
to her?

Was his use of 32 languages a means of evasion
whenever she leaned into his heart?

He honored black Americans, money for freedom;
how did he honor Native Americans?
Did he honor his family, smiles for questions?

He invented languages, defined the universe,
fought for the reformation of society.
So much to do, so little time —
Vacuity in the center of bedlam.

When he returned home after 2 am meetings
to change language, the world,
was his faith so great, so clear, so consistent,
that he also wanted to change his family, himself?
Or did his reformations slough off at the bedroom door?

Duty above all was the center of that time.
Did Stephen when he woke each morning
to thunder his beliefs to anyone who cared to listen,
listen to his children's butterflies, spinning tops, music boxes?
Did he cock his head as his wife rustled the sheets
next to him, her lips silently mouthing dreams?

Mountain Goats

The heft and heave of goats scrambling up slopes
       and cliffs of Lake Okanagan,
cloven hooves gripping granite ice.

We chased them—the mountain-goat caller,
his voice ringing the goats,
asking permission for the goats to give their lives.

Bolting up the rocks, the goats wavered
between the hunters at the base,
and those above—
bows drawn,
fingers knocked against the arrow shafts.

Calls broke rocks that spiralled into space,
sending the hunters scrambling for safety.

But the goats locked into line.

Finally, *Stla-Chain-Um*, she of the deer family,
her voice the voice of goats,
spoke through her throat, her gravel words
shaking the goats from their trance to continue their run
       along the cliffs.
Goats for food,
stories for children and generations.
The hard scrape of flesh against red-streaked rocks,
broken bones mixed with the hunt's excitement.

Clutching for life onto rocks
rubbed smooth by generations of goats,
like the great buffalo stones of the plains.

We traded life for life.

Free fall, the abrupt loss of weight
for a few moments
of drift before everything switches off,
no gap between the whistle and impact,
no gap between life and death.

After,
the feast
and the red stars
bright with the pupils of goats.

Untitled

I awoke in the early morning and walked towards the public transit station. Troy's brother offered me a ride home. I accepted. He turned off the highway into an industrial area. I asked him where he was going, he replied that he had to pick up some papers from work first. Once we parked he stated that he was going to have sex with me. I laughed and told him he wasn't. We were in a deserted parking lot on a Sunday morning; he was twice my weight and size. He proceeded to rape me despite my tears, protests. I told him that I would pee on him. He threatened that if I knew what was good for me I wouldn't.

A while later the Creator intervened. Before the rapist was to sodomize me a truck pulled into the parking lot. The man in the truck went into the building—he was too far away to hear any screaming. The rapist's attitude changed. He said he would now drive me home. I stayed in the back seat while he drove. Before leaving the parking lot I memorized the truck driver's license plate number and later wrote it down. I didn't know why. I told the rapist that I still had to use the washroom.'" He drove to the nearest gas station. As I got out and walked around the car I memorized the rapist's license plate number. He got the key for the washroom and I went in and quickly scribbled a note stating that I had been raped and the rapist was driving me home. I put down my address, the type and colour of the rapist's car and his license plate number. I brought the key inside the gas station and gave the note to the cashier. I got back in the rapist's car and we proceeded to my place. The police pulled up to the car when the rapist stopped his vehicle near my home. They ordered me to get away from the car and the rapist to get out with his hands up. Music to my ears.

Since I hadn't known the area where I was raped, I told the officer about the truck that pulled in and that I had taken his license plate number down. They were able to track down the location with that information. God helped me through this ordeal. But, it was only the beginning.

I skipped school and spent the next two weeks huddled in my basement suite. I found it difficult to concentrate upon returning to school. It would take time for me to get my GPA back to where it had been.

The trial was nearly a year and a half later. I planned to put the ordeal to the back of my mind until after the trial. I didn't begin the healing process until after the trial. I didn't want to think about it.

The rape took place in Vancouver, B.C. I moved to the Okanagan four months after the trial to get away from the bad memories. I moved with my boyfriend. I had no other friends or relatives in the Okanagan.

I tried to run away from my problems. I began to feel lost, helpless and depressed. I felt I was going to crack. I cried out in anguish in my boyfriend's arms. He could do little to put my mind at ease. The pain was so unbearable that I was having anguished crying fits in the middle of the day or any other given time. Old wounds were re-opening.

I phoned my step-mom. She had been my mother since the age of six, I was glad she was there for me. I was feeling anger towards my step-mom. She had abused my brother and I almost immediately after my mother's death. I don't remember what I said to her on the phone. I was crying and feeling helpless; she told me it was okay to feel the anger towards her. She also informed me that my old emotional wounds would re-open. She was correct. Somehow her understanding comforted me. My healing was just beginning. I went for a walk along a wooded creek area nearly a month later. I was feeling depressed. I prayed to our Creator to give me relief from my grief. Seconds later I looked down at the over-flowing, turbulent creek and saw two ducks. The mallard looked behind at his female counterpart, I figured to make certain she was unharmed. It was so-o-o cute. I laughed aloud happily. There was my sign from our Creator that everything was going to be okay. A few months later I got a job as the First Nation Education Coordinator's Assistant. From this job I learned plenty about my heritage. My spirit was growing stronger each day.

Unfortunately, shortly after I started working, the strain on my relationship with my boyfriend was too much. He was having problems of his own and needed to focus on them wholly. We mutually decided to go our separate ways. During our relationship he helped me get in touch with who I was. Before we had started going out I had dreamed of working in New York as a tough business woman. I had figured I would be happy down there. Nothing could have been further from the truth. He helped me get back in touch with my naturalist side. I love fishing, camping and hiking. We loved doing these activities together.

I went to my first powwow a couple of months into my job. I accompanied my mentor to the pow wow representing our school. I was captivated. The event was over-powering with spirituality, culture and camaraderie. I participated in a dance, with a little coaxing from my mentor, and like a child I wanted more. I went to another pow wow a couple of months later. Like the first one I had gone to, the dancers' regalia were spectacular and colourful. The variations of dance were all mesmerizing. The arbor was breathtaking. It was rumoured to be the finest in America. I was overwhelmed with how we all came together in celebration of family, unity, understanding, warmth, peace, joy, life, song, dance, drumming, Mother Earth, and our Creator.

Karen Coutlee

Child Inside

Oh precious child inside
Look at me now little girl
I wish you peace now
It's safe to play now.

Stay with me little girl
I need you now little girl
I feel so lost and alone
I feel so hurt inside.

Stay with me little girl
No need to hide anymore
Look at me now little girl
Please come out and trust me.

I wish you all the best
I love you now and forever
I will be here for you
Do not be afraid little girl.

Look at your Elders
Look at your parents
Look at your sister
And look at your brother.

Come out and look at me
We can be strong little girl
Oh precious child inside
It's safe to sleep tonight.

I need to play and laugh
I need to live and feel
We need to cry and rage
We need to move along.

Look at me now little girl
I will not push you away
I will not hurt you
I am your friend now.

We are the Eagle
We are the living tree
We are the little stream
We are the wind and rain.

We are from Mother Earth
I honour you little girl
I give you freedom
So look at me now little girl.

Come out and look at life
We don't have time to waste
Come out and dance and sing
Give your troubles to the wind.

Stay with me little girl
We belong to the Creator
We are protected now
I wish you all of life.

Celebration

MariJo Moore

To Celebrate Not Explain The Mystery

And I heard a voice
a silvery voice wrapped
in secrets of red and purple

telling me to go deep, deep inside myself
deep to the deepest part where the light lay
in the centre of the darkness

that it would be here
I would find the celebration
of who I am, why I exist,
where I come from and where I am going

and in this celebration I would find
the explanation that requires no explaining
the knowledge that requires no knowing
the answer that requires no questioning

and then I would understand
and I would not understand
and then it would not matter.

Karenne Wood

Celebrating Corn

Rhythmic pounding of
pestle against the
white stone
> *I have planted my corn*

she grinds last year's harvest to meal.
A thin white-gold powder clings to her
hands. Around her, air shimmers.
> *I have planted it with my song*

One of the
puppies is barking; its staccato
yap yap punctuates her quick strokes.
> *Let it grow tall and beautiful*

Beside her, an aunt stitches
shell beads to deerskin. Her nieces
lean toward clay pots to stir embers.
> *watered by rains*

The young men are gathering new
clay for ochre. Beyond domed
bark houses, fields
> *washed in sunlight*

stretch small earthen mounds toward the river.
Redbuds blossom, their branches upturned like hands to
receive the sky's sacraments.
> *corn and squash, blessed by waters*

She pats meal into ashcakes. Already
dusk comes; a smell of bread rises. Painted, the
men drum their song.
> *Grandmother, we plant our seeds*

For a thousand years now,
for a thousand years after, her people
dance when redbuds bloom
> *celebrating corn.*

Jack Forbes

The Oldest Path

Growing older is a path
worn smooth by the
unending tread of travellers,
even the stony places
now worn down to polished smoothness

But perhaps
there is no single path,
for some age-travellers
follow trails of high adventure,
each mile adding something new,
while for others
the trail is one of loss
each mile seeing
something gone,
Some other thing
that one can no longer do

And then again
maybe it is one single path after all
but only one's seeing of it varies,
some remarking only on things lost
others noticing only the new
and some discovering a
joy in reflecting on
things past,
on moments gone
which, strangely, still return.

Growing older is a path
worn smooth by the
unending tread of travellers—
grandfathers and grandmothers
have gone before
mothers and fathers as well
to that doorway
where our *nchichank*
our that-which-separates
finds a new *muhtomakan*
a new road
and a new beginning.

94

The Quest

Am I on a quest, or did I get off the trail
　　　for a quest is demanding, consuming
　　　or is it rest not quest that I seek
　　　an interim between jerks of seeking
　　　but seeking that is easy, not too hard
　　　no Holy Grail for me with unfriendly dragons
　　　and hostile warriors to test my mettle?

But then I've already done battle many times
　　　the enemies remember me well though
　　　some have grown old and their hard lines of
　　　opposition have melted with irrelevance
　　　since I go on fighting on different battlefields
　　　choosing my weapons and my place
　　　when I can!

Young people are here to take over some of those
　　　trails and I give them cheers, advice and
　　　warnings of twists and turns
　　　while I dig deeper into the reality of my few years
　　　left in this incarnation
　　　needing moments of reflection to find the *mutomaakan*
　　　the road for these years
　　　but pausing to rest—
　　　is that distraction or a loss of direction
　　　or just my 64th year from the womb

For the battle for wisdom is every much demanding as the fight
　　　for justice, the quest for truth and fair play, which I have tried
　　　to be following for two score and more years and it
　　　still has me in its firm grip
　　　as I seek at the same time to pass the baton
　　　to young men and women
　　　not to become lazy but to get on to that other
　　　quest, the wisdom road

Of course, maybe old men and women like to seek wisdom because
        it gives one the excuse of sitting quietly a lot, sort of day
        dreaming perhaps or remembering old times
        not actually getting
        very far into nirvana, but
        my quest is an active one where wisdom is based upon
        acts and acts are, I hope, based upon wisdom
        and they feed into one another

When did my quests begin?
        when I emerged from my mother
        reluctantly
        after hours and even days
        of my dear mother's labour, and was I afraid to leave
        that warm and liquid place?
        or perhaps it was only that I was in a difficult spot
        unable to come forth easily
        is that the source of some of my deepest fears?

My mother, precious mother Dorothy, had a tilted uterus,
        was not supposed to be able to give birth
        but she told me how the great earthquake of 1933
        shook her up and she finally became pregnant
        So an earthquake made it all possible, and for that I
        give thanks to Mother Earth, *Gaaheseena Haakee*

Indeed, I feel that I am on a quest, that my life
        especially these past few years
        is part of a seeking, that it is
        surely a questing . . . or questings

When I run I like to feel that I am on a seeking,
        in new places through forests on narrow trails
        or along the edge of the ocean between rocks
        and cliff, looking eagerly near and above for
        each journey is a seeking after connections
        with boulders and birds
        with plants and special pebbles

with wind and waves, and clouds and creeks
ancient peat bogs and old glass floats from Japan
each journey a new exploration
along old or new paths, each trip
made new by its complete uniqueness
in the stream of time

Young babies, young children, are on the discovery path
    "Hey Dad, give me the big picture please"
    as they seek for meaning, for understanding
    who they are, who they are not,
    of what they are to be in relation to
    mother, father, dog, cat, sister, brother
    where do they end?
    where do they begin?

Later they dream of planets and milky ways
        of fates and destinies, and
        infinite possibilities
        then, as one grows older one returns
        perhaps to that search for meaning,
        to know, "who am I?"
        "where do I begin?"
        "where do I end?"
        "where did I come from?'
        "where am I going next?"

Some of us want to know "why have I lived,
        have I left a mark, have I loved enough,
        touched enough people, with jewels of caring,
        with treasures of affection?"

Seeking also to come to an understanding of death
        and birth and rebirth, with growth and decay
        hoping for the spring that follows every winter
        when the plants come up again
        that is the old Native American way

to gain the strength which is wisdom
to know how to live in a world which
changes constantly like the dunes on the beach
and which takes away from us
our youth, our maturity
and our dearest loved ones
our dearest friends and then takes us away as well

How should one live such a life as we have?
        my quest, my seeking is the same
        as that of all of the Old Ones
        to take my place in the long line
        of the ones who have gone before
        along this same well-worn path
        which at the same time may be new and fresh
        for those who travel without a guide

Still, I am attached to this life
        for my strength comes from Mother Earth, *Gaaheseena Haakee,*
        and from my friends the trees, the clouds
        all my relations indeed
        and the Great Rock Tosaut on the beach
        my good friend to whom I say *waanishee!*
        and the wind and fog
        and the humans whom I love
        and all of this I find so liberating
        just so know these gifts of *keeshaylemokong,*
        Creator of us all

And I still quest for justice and fairplay and truth
        with poems and books and research
        In historical documents and ancient books
        and people's stories
        the songs of birds
        and I am not ready to abandon
        this road which I have been on

But it will come, it seems, that time when
      I will set aside what has been
      and leave the familiar road behind
      setting off on new *mutomaakana*
      unknown to me now

Still, my quest will not be solitary even then
      For I have learned that animals, trees
      and plants, clouds and mountains
      friends and lovers
      indeed the beautiful universe
      make me complete and eliminate my boundaries
      stretching me to the stars

Our quests
      no matter on what road
      must bring us closer still
      to our true nature
      which is not one of escape or soledad
      but one of belonging to all that is,
      was and ever will be

Untitled

To: Leah George Wilson, Joe Thomas, Bob George & others

There isn't a word for what some people do,
some people are born artists
or leaders
or those who help with grief
but others are those who bind,
connect people with warmth,
throw out a web
to catch those of us
who might get lost otherwise—
they are health
in a sometimes frightened community,
they are on both sides in any dispute.
Maybe there is a word for them
in some of our languages.
They are in all our communities
nourishing us
and could be called
the Purveyors of Love.

Ravens

Influenced by the writing of Pema Chodron in, The Wisdom of No Escape.

I receive my inspiration
from ravens
fearless and joyful,
their tattered black wings
goofily spread,
feet and beaks
hanging onto branches
while gale winds
ruffle feathers
swing them backwards
and they just let go
dropping helter skelter
into the wind
enjoying the wildness
of the weather,
not knowing where
it's going to take them
or what will happen next.
They catch each others feet,
free fall
then fly out like airplanes.
They meet challenges
with zest
and make them into play.
Crows and ravens,
you can see them
everywhere.

Vera M. Wabegijig

Deeply Breathing

insisting on breathing deeply
moist earth
of fresh dew
clinging creation
natural sweetgrass
enters my essence

insisting on breathing deeply
warm summer breeze
pollen collects
in my hair
flowering
begins at roots
giving way
to new life

insisting on breathing deeply
memories that gather
braiding
in my hair
glimpses into
past present future
making new paths
for new generations

insisting on breathing deeply
cedar tree branches
falling down
on soft hands
rubbing away
stress in dark limbs
recycling,
into cedar roots

insisting on breathing deeply
winds carry songs from east
beating into earth,
connecting to heart
feet pulse
on sweet grass

rhythm awakens
spirit's song

insisting on breathing deeply
new awakenings
beginnings

just insisting
on breathing deeply
each and every time.

my granny inspired me

when i was a little girl . . .
with my thick black hair
my skin was brown as wet mud pies under the beaming rays of
sun in july
i didn't wear much except for a pair of underwear
i spent most of my time outside or

sitting having tea with my granny

all the while all of my cousins were out running around on the
reserve i loved visiting my granny on the reserve ... which was
only weekends or almost all of the summertime   i was between
five and seven   i sat beside my granny on her right-hand side of
her favourite chair

and her favourite table in the kitchen   she'd tell me stories about
my mom when she was young, about all my uncles and aunties
about her life back in wiki and how it was when she married my
grandfather and moved to his reserve, mississauga

in 1917, my granny was married   she was only seventeen then
she moved to my grandpa's reserve   nobody liked her because she
was odawa:kwe   and from wikwemikong,   manitouland island
this did not stop her from trying though   she raised seven children
and had the only farm on that reserve

my grandpa died in the sixties   i don't know much about him
only that he was a good man and one of my brothers is named
after him   i still hear stories about him, my grandma calls him, old
Charlie

he made my favourite swing outside my granny's house, its tied
up to an old red pine tree   it's still there today and he made my
granny's house
my granny's stories were mostly told in odawa, which is very sim-
ilar to ojibway, they were about her life: her struggles   her good

times   her hard times   her family   what she learned most in this life
and how beautiful life is

she loved life   she encouraged me to go out and have an adventure   she always knew how to have a good time no matter what she was doing or where she was   one of her favourite things to do was have people over at her house and have some beers

after she felt good, i remember my granny pulling out her harmonica and my uncle his guitar and they would play music and sing   then my granny would start to dance   tap dancing and two steppin'   her favourite song was, roll out the barrel:
>... roll out the barrel
>roll out the barrel of fun
>roll out the barrel
>we'll have a barrel of fun ...

on her ninetieth birthday the reserve had a big birthday party for her   she got up and sang roll out the barrel   i think that was one of the last times she sang that song

when she smiled her wrinkles were so beautiful and when she laughed her whole body jiggled with delight   i can still hear her laughing...

after she died in 1993, i couldn't remember all of this   i couldn't speak of her

now i celebrate her life

i celebrate my memories of her
i celebrate her stories she shared with me

i remember her today as i write this   she taught me so much about being anishnawbe:kwe   it is her roots that i follow when i write my stories, my poems   i connect all memories with her   she has inspired me to do what   i am doing now   following my dreams

Vera M. Wabegijig

and now, as all of our stories come to me i write for my nephew
and nieces . . . and my unborn child   i write for all creation, and all
the many generations to come

when i want to remember more . . .
i sit outside and look to the east . . . my home
and dream of that little girl . . . that i once was
sitting beside my granny sipping tea and eating scones
laughing and talking in anishnawbe.

Tahltan

Shimmering moon on sparkling water,
Dance pretty flower
Mother Natures' daughter.
Shimmering rocks on a river bed,
Indian paintbrush
Paint my world red
While clouds like fluff
walk under our sun,
Yellow and orange for everyone.
Jump silver salmon and
growl little bear.
I'll let the breeze blow
through my black hair.
With my eyes open wide
I catch everything:
Every dance, every sparkle,
Every bird singing.
My ears can't believe
what my eyes see,
and my heart beats alive
to these wondrous things.
The sheep on the mountains
blend with the snow,
Fireweed follows me
wherever I go.
I gaze over the land,
the land that's our home.
Tahltan.

We Go Forward

We are still here,
laughing and singing, giving
birth to babies and ideas.

We dance at wedding celebrations
and over invisible borders, our faces
fitting perfectly along the landscape.

Our grandchildren speak words
and tell stories risen from pond
bottoms and tree stumps, thought

to be brackish or cut down. Songs
which rattled around in museums
echo from Passamaquoddy to Penticton.

We are on the front line, healing
in shiny clinics, defending in polished
courtrooms, teaching in universities.

What have we lost on the way?
My grandmother says the better question
has to be "where are we headed?"

Virgin Dance

The old people gathered in grandmother's house
They drank tea and talked about long ago
The time of floods, and great salmon runs
Old Frank picked up his drum
His eyes looked sad and finally they closed shut
His drumbeat summoned the spirits
The old women began to sing, their voices somber
Grandmother nudged me to get up and dance!
Fear shook my bone: I never danced before
I don't know how to dance!
I rose to my feet
The old people were in a trance
My heart beat hard
Sounds in the room echoed through my ears
My feet began to move
Suddenly, spirits surrounded my body
And invaded my mind
I was no longer part of the earth
No longer human
The spirits took me into the other world

Montanna Rose

My little mountain rose
so fragrant and sweet.
You are as gentle as the summer's breeze.
Pink lips the shade of petals.
A smile as radiant as the sun,
Your chatter is like a babbling brook.
A kindness as sturdy as the stem of a rose
little temper as sharp as the thorns.

Eight winters,
eight summers
have come and gone
you've given me smiles
when mine are tired.
You nudge me awake
when the best part
of the fairytale is on.
You share your
strawberry sundaes with me
when mine is gone.
We've laughed and cried together
through good times and bad.

I want you to know...
you were my life line
when I thought I was drowning.
You were my pillar of strength
when I was weak with sorrow
You broke the chains of hate
I had wrapped around my heart.
This relationship is not
bound by anything
    but
        heartstrings.

    I love you Montanna Rose.
I offer you this letter poem
to celebrate your birth,
and your growth.
To celebrate your teaching me
to be a good mother, friend and person.

My Life is a Tobacco Tie

My life is a tobacco tie,
a sacred offering every morning
to the water spirits who named me,
a sacred offering
with a place in the sweat lodge,
a shred of the bounty of the land
wrapped in red,
a way to send thoughts
to the Creator,
a way to honour
my grandfathers and grandmothers,
a way to give thanks that
my life is a tobacco tie.

Lois Red Elk

Building A Fire

We all have our own way
of building a fire.
We start with dried grasses,
carefully pile on cottonwood
kindling, point the small
branch tips toward the center,
and lay slow burning logs
on top.
We rub stone against flint,
spark a light, blow on the
embers, urge out small flames,
red energy grows and leaps
into life.
We watch dark faces glow,
eyes reflect a drum, everyone
sings, is happy. We become
one as we reach for warmth.
Unattended the fire could
go out, so we prepared, we
watched, we lit tobacco,
we promised to keep seven
campfires burning.
We never thought our fires
would be smothered, never
dreamed how quiet the night,
but we did dream of a dawn
with no light, our children
with spotted bodies, animals
with only three legs, woke
up confused.

We found our grandparents
dead, no one greeted the
day, our fires began to go
out-one by one, we thought
our Gods had died.

We stumbled on one small
twig smoldering quietly
remembered dried sweet grass,
found our spirits along the
way, heard our words turn
into new songs.
That raging light in the east
took pity on us, lent courage
to our ashes, a wind danced
for our coals, broken limbs
began to gather from distant
woods and once again, in
abundance, we roared.
This is one of the stories
we will tell. We'll always
remember sound without the
crackle of flame, without
the laughter of the old ones.
And, with stronger, tendered,
red voices we will tell the
children to dream, to sing,
to pray, to tend to the last
coal, tell of the time fire
taught us to build our lives
so we would never die out.

The Rabbit Story
(Traditional)

A little rabbit went out to walk on a cool day in the Fall. Oh, it was real cool.

And he came to a willow tree, and so he began to dance around and around. Well, by and by the wind came to a willow tree, and he began to shiver. "Oh, it's kinda cool."

So he danced faster and faster around the willow tree. After a while he looked up into the sky, and he said, "I think it's going to snow."

By and by it did snow. So he danced faster and faster around the willow tree and patted the snow all down.

By and by he became so tired that he sat down on a limb of the willow tree and went to sleep.

He slept so long that when he awoke all the snow had melted and down below was all green.

Now you know the rabbit is a very timid animal. He was sitting up in the willow tree and he was afraid to jump out of a tree.

He was very hungry. He shut his eyes up tight and fell right out of that tree.

When he did, he cut his upper lip on a sharp stone. Now every rabbit has a split upper lip.

But when he fell out of that tree, he jammed his front legs right up into his body.

Now every single rabbit and every single Easter Bunny has two short legs.

But when he fell out of that tree, it caught his tail and now every single rabbit has a short tail.

Now, when you're driving through the country in the Spring next year, and you come to a willow tree and think you're picking pussy willows . . . you'll know why all the little Indian children know that's where the rabbit left his tail on the willow tree.

Unnehtongquat Papaume Mohtukquasemes

Pasuk kesuk adt 'ninnauwaet mohtukquasemes quequeshau. Ho moocheke tohkoi.

Peyau yean anumwussukuppe. Pumukau mehtugq waeenu kah waeenu. Teanuk waban ootshoh. Sonkquesu. Wussin, "nus-sonkques"

Popomshau mehtuhq nano. Naim ushpuhquaeu kesukquieu. Wussin, "Pish muhpoo"

Naim muhpooi. Pumukau moocheke waeenu kah waeenu anumwussukuppe. Togkodtam muhpoo manunne.

Naim sauunum onk tohkootaau mehtugq yeuyeu onk kussukkoueu. Koueu noadtuk. Tookshau. Muhpoo mohtupohteau. Quinnupohke ashashki.

Noh wahteunk mohtukquasog, wahheau naag na sohqutteah-hauhaog. Nagum nont qushitteaonk. Mat queshau wutche mehtukq. Paskanontam. Yanunum wuskesukquash onk queshau wutche mehtukq.

Tiadche petshau kenompskut. Wussissetoon kuhkukque musqueheongane. Yeuyeu nishnoh mohtukquas mahche pohki kuhkukque mussisstoon-mahche neese kuhkukque mussis-stoonash.

Asuh ahquompak kepshont wusseettash waapemooash adt wuhhog. Yeuyeu nishnoh mohtukquas onk nishnoh "Easter Bunny" mahche neese tiohquekekontash.

Aoog adt touohkomuk onk nok wompiyeuash dtannetuog ut anumwussukuppe nummukkiog Indiansog newutche mohtugquasemesog wussukqunnash.

Kesteausu

(Translated by Authors Strong Woman and Moondancer)

Land, Relationship and Community

Land, terra firma, solid, expansive, holy.

Before land there was nothing, only a void was there, a darkness.

The *"raison d'etre"* for all of life did not exist, and therefore neither did reason, the contemplative, or story.

According to the cosmology of my ancestors, the Rock Cree, first there was *Whey-sa-keh-chak*, the trickster, the first man.

Then there was the back of the turtle, then there was the muskrat; and then, and only then, there was the land.

The muskrat was delegated to dive deep into the murky void of the first water, and find if possible, a sign of the existence of land.

The muskrat, being credible to the task and being oily enough, thus full-filled her mandate, expiring in the process, but nonetheless surfacing, clutching in her webbed little paw, a miniscule portion of real estate.

Before that there was nothing but a great blackness and immense space, not even a solar system, much less time.

The Rock Cree of the pre-Cambrian Shield's boreal region of Canada are trappers and hunters; gatherers of roots and medicine, and fishers of lakes and river systems as ancient as *Whey-sa-keh-chak*.

I, the son of shamans and medicine men, the progeny of pagans, I am of the land and the land (*Aski*) is the marrow of my bone.

My first relationship with land was as a newborn whereby my mother swaddled me in a diaper of dried moss called *Aski*, earth.

My dad, born on the trapline, was to be cleansed in the snow, his first blood mingling with the land forever.

Much as the platinum infused nickel ore of my homeland, my essence also is buried deep within the permafrost.

Back home there is an ancient language, an old way of speaking (kyas-*seh-thin-ne-mo-win)*, a "Classic Cree" as it were.

It is a language which only the very elderly use now if at all, plus some not so old who were raised by grandparents.

What is unique about this "Classic Cree" is that the whole of the idiom pertains to and concerns itself with landscape, to specificity of place, and to one's relationship to the land.

Classic Cree is a precise and economic language, colorful and poetic in its speaking.

Ee-es-pas-que-yak, means a stand of tall and sparcely spaced tamarack running from a lower ground level, and sloping up to a higher terrain.

It is a language for the passionate and those that need to take great chunks of life and beauty with a full feeling in the breast.

It is large and spacious and constant like the powerful land from which it derives.

In autumn there is a profusion of color when leaves and sky will appropriate a Tom Thompson.

There is a Rock Cree word for how one feels in the heart gazing upon such a panorama.

It is a language made for the observant, not the talkative.

When I speak to you in Cree, I acknowledge you as community.

When the land speaks to me she acknowledges me as community.

I can well appreciate the fact that it's very difficult for the Western mind (the English speaking mind, if you will) to comprehend the notion of land speaking, as if it were alive.

The inadequate Canadian education system does not give one the flexibility of "holistic thought," as the Rock Cree know it, as a paradigm.

It does not have that kind of sophistication.

Learn from me, listen to me; the land is speaking.

Language, whether classic Cree or contemporary Cree is the basis of our community.

How we speak and why we speak formulates, shapes, dictates and drives the engine of essence (who we are) and landscape (where we are).

In fact the Plains Cree word for Cree Nation translates into "a Cree speaker."

We ask each other on first meeting, "Are you a Cree speaker?"

"Are you one of us, do you speak the language, are you of our community?"

It is inconceivable and devoid of reason to the Cree Mind that language should not address both the land and community.

The power of land as an agent of life can never be refuted by a Rock Cree, especially a trapper.

To this very day, back home, when an old trapper would succumb to illness, or fall into disease, he will ask a grandchild to transport him "to his land," *o-tas-keihk.*

After an appropriate period he will return to the community completely recovered.

We say he has had a relationship not "to" but "with" the land, *e-kit-tim-ah-kon-a-kot-aski,* "The land has taken pity on him".

Once more the land has sustained his breath.

The going about the the world as a living human being is called, *Pim-mat-tis-se-win;* it suggests the totality of all life as a relationship with self.

Like Sandra Semchuk, my wife, likes to say, "with self and with other."

We see ourselves as holistic beings, not separate entities whereby the whole may be deduced as the total sum of its parts ... Land, relationship and community is not an issue of separateness but a question of balance, between equal and complete universes.

When I was a kid church was a very big deal in the lives of our families. My dad, a medicine man, was also a lay churchperson.

Of course the priest was always ecstatic at the weekly turn-out of Indians at his doorstep.

Unbeknownst to the poor chap was the reason for such a fiesty congregation is the Cree's penchant for socialization and the bringing together of community.

Any reason to get together and have a few good laughs!

The occasions of Sunday were usually marked by pre-mass chit-chat and gossip, regardless of weather, and post-mass visiting and politics.

Then the merrymaking would really get into high gear.

Everybody would abscond to the lakeshore and campfires would ablaze all around, while the ladies laid out lunch at high noon.

Everyone would cater to their respective peer groups; the ladies cooking, the men talking politics of church and state, and we the kids swimming and carrying on as best we could.

Oh, it was a holy and processional event, an epiphany most reserved for the savage breast!

I always remember the padre mingling among his converted, "the shepherd tending to his sheep" all awash in black cassock, pausing here and there to chat in atrocious Cree, but happy.

There were many good human beings among the priesthood. One of my best friends certainly was.

I have deconstructed much from the church, but these words remain valid: "Remember o man thou art dust and unto dust thou shall return."

To all things old and to all things new, the Cree would entrench anew the notion of community, re-invent community.

Land is the source of all life and the last indictment of all substance having existed.

I am fascinated by the image of giant yellow pieces of "tonka toy" machinery, discarded in its' rusting hulkiness, oxidizing in quiet isolation.

Maybe a tree growing through it's spokes, as it dies abandoned, victimized by time and economics.

How can, I ask an object so immense, so invincible, so inconquerable, at last turn to a mere handful of rust; albeit after a millennia or so.

Everything goes back to the earth, time ravages everything and everyone for all time; from the great pyramid to the littlest ant chasing it's own frenzy at the edge of her world.

Opportunities for Growth

Waiting for inspiration on the topic for this year's *Gatherings* I came upon many things that would lead me to believe that there are very few who are "Beyond Victimization" or 'Forging a Path to Celebration." I speak mainly of the year that is just beginning and the opportunity I have had to pray for many people who are not yet walking towards that gift from the Creator. I guess because I am in University that I am seeing many things that I would not have had the opportunity to see, had I been in the working world.

As a person in recovery who worked in the field for many years I experienced only that which pertained to the healing and recovery of addictions and abuses. I read only literature pertaining to that field and paid little attention to the "sections" that this university has dissected life. I never paid attention to separating people according to lifestyle, gender, class, etc. I worked with people who were asking for help, no matter who they were.

As a grad student in American Studies I've learned a tremendous amount about people and their biases, prejudices, and of course racism. What I'm finding is that no matter who you are you may have some or all of these "afflictions." I say that facetiously. What I mean is that I found in a Women's Studies course that some of the women were more concerned with classism and were not open to learning about others. In my Native Studies classes I found a lot of prejudices.

Now you may say that this is quite normal. Well maybe it is and then maybe we need to look at "normal." I would like it to not be normal for people to judge others based on their ability to get jobs, or to work for a living. I would like to see it be normal for people to accept others not for their skin color but because they are humans. I would like to see people start to get along, but that doesn't seem like it is too near in the future.

Celebrating our Resilience seems to be a better way of looking at things. I see the resilience of Native People in North America for they have survived every kind of annihilation and assimilation to date. I'm not sure that they will for very much longer because of the government infiltration and the "sleeping with the enemy" type actions on the part of the entrepreneurs who seem to "know what is best" for the communities.

Our people have survived the addictions, compulsions, and exploitations but we must remember so have others.

Right now, in Central and South America, as well as Mexico our relatives are being murdered, jailed, tortured, raped, and everything else that happened to our ancestors here in North America many years ago. I don't believe that we can say that we have moved "beyond victimization" yet or until all our relatives are safe. Yes we are more advanced; we are more modern; could you say more assimilated than those in the other countries?

The non-Indigenous people in the governments and corporations are still exploiting, and cannot see that the people are connected to the earth. They do not see that when you kill one or destroy one you destroy the other. As we move into the next few years how many of our people will join in destroying the land, the homelands and the people.

I'm trying very hard to stay away from the gambling and the taxation and land issues that plague our communities but I'm afraid they are all related to the destruction of the people. They are all related to the destruction of the traditional ways. No, I'm not a proponent of the "going back to the old ways" ideas. I'm promoting "bringing the teachings forward."

I believe that the education of our "little trees" needs to take place in the communities. Yes that was a play on words. The *Education of Little Tree* was a book that I read back in 1990. I found it had some very good points. What I remember was that the little boy was educated in many ways by his grandfather and grandmother. When he was taken away and put in the boarding school he had those teachings to rely on when he was suffocating in that place . . . Educating our "little trees," the children, can take place in our communities. It can take place in our schools if need be when the parents are so assimilated that they don't have the teachings themselves.

No not everyone was raised in the traditional way in our communities but do they have to be to get the traditional teachings? The messages in any "man made religions" have a basic premise the same as all traditional teachings. That message is "Above all else it is love, respect, and truth." Love the Creator first. Love all people as if they were the Creator in front of you. Respect everything and everyone because they were made by the Creator and therefore are part of the Creator. Treat everyone and everything with that respect that you have for the Creator. And truth. Always tell the truth because every thought word and deed is a communication with the Creator.

When I think of Celebrating I think of our dances, our songs, and our ceremonies and I think of the prayers that we have for ourselves. I would ask that as we celebrate in song, dance, ceremony and prayer that we give thanks for the people that are part of this world that don't have the opportunities. Those people were robbed of their traditions and ceremonies long, long ago before they came to our lands. They may not always have good intentions but when we continue to fight them we are continuing the negativity that is permeating this world. That negativity is destroying the very air we breathe and the water we drink.

I would propose that we give thanks for the opportunity to experience the things that we do for, without them we would not know good. In our teachings we have the Twins as many other cultures do. We can think of them as the Good Twin and the Evil Twin but why not give them different names. Why not think of them as Balance. Left and Right. Darkness and Light. Wrong and Right. Whatever name you choose think of it as balance. Whenever we come across a problem be thankful that we have an opportunity to think of a way to accomplish something new.

This opportunity to pray for people here at the University is not because I'm so "holier than thou" as some people would say. It is because I've run into some doozies. I pray for the person who viciously attacks the people who are trying to do good work because that person couldn't have his own way. I pray for the administration who doesn't think about the students and their well being but of the corporations that want to give big money.

I pray for the people who are lost there and don't know yet that the way to happiness is inside and not out there with the mega-bucks. I pray for the ones who are still suffering with the alcohol, drugs, gambling, food, work, sex, relationships and all the rest of the addictions. I pray for the ones who are suffering with the diseases of diabetes, heart disease and all of the rest of the diseases that are here to destroy. I give thanks and pray that you all are Celebrating your Resilience and moving Beyond Victimization.

Youth

The Drought and The Thunder Bird

It was another hot summer day. The sun was beating down on the dry creek beds. We were in the midst of a serious drought. There were few salmon coming from the river. Our village can't live like this any longer. The Chief talked to the elders and decided to send young *Tuu-tii-ʔin-ukʼs* up in to the mountains. There she would find the secret medicine to burn in the great fire to call upon the great Thunder Bird.

She started her journey at first light and got there at night fall. She set up camp and asked the Creator for guidance for what needed to be done. She woke up at first light and searched for the secret medicine. She found the medicine by the beds of the dried up creek. She began the ceremony to call upon the great Thunder Bird. She finished by first light and waited for the great Thunder Bird's appearance.

The great Thunder Bird was perched in his cave and heard the cry of the two-leggeds. He began his quest to the village. She heard his wings as he neared. "Swoosh, swoosh." The sky turned dark and lightning flashed in the sky and the thunder rumbled so loudly that it shook the earth. Rain came down in torrents and filled up the creeks, nourishing the two and four-leggeds.

Tuu-tii-ʔin-ukʼs thanked the Thunder Bird for bringing the rains. She began the trip to the village. As she looked down on our village she saw everyone dancing in the rain. Everyone was happy again, life had been restored.

A Blank Spot In Me

My auntie was a nice person. She would bring us to the store and other places. She would let us get stuff and she would pay for it. She used to always make me happy when I was sad. She would let me stay up all night when it was a school night. She would take us swimming in the summer.

But that can't happen any more because one day I heard that she died. So now whenever I think of her, a big blank spot inside me gets bigger. So I have to try to fill the blank spot with happiness.

Blank Spot In My Head

I sit here thinking of what to write. Staring at a blank piece of paper sitting in front of my face. Tapping my pencil on my desk, just thinking of what to write. Nothing's coming out of my mind. I'm getting frustrated! My teacher's telling me to stay in my seat. Every one is talking, they are getting me confused. There's a boy singing in the corner, being a loner. There's a girl over there, talking on the phone for about the twentieth time today! There's a boy sitting in his desk trying to get an A. My friend is drinking her juice, trying to make sure the teacher doesn't see her. Some days school can really, really SUCK!

I Remember

I remember when my Mom was drunk.
I remember when my Dad died.
I remember when I was mad.
I remember when everyone was mad at me.
I remember when I was mad at my Mom.
I remember when everyone was liking me.
I remember when my Mom didn't care about me.
I remember when my Dad didn't love me.
I remember where I'm going to be.

Butterfly

Freedom has many exotic colours
that light up the darkness
and darken the brightness.
Colours that change in the sunlight
Colours that change in the moonlight
Special colours for you and me
and drab colours for the rest of the world.

Freedom has many amazing patterns
with step designs to represent acceleration
and round edge designs to signify compassion
and arrow designs to form direction
and razor sharp designs to enhance strength
and straight edge designs to comprehend logic.

Freedom has many spontaneous pathways,
that lead into a forest of complete comfort,
and into a metropolis of unlimited adventures,
and into a countryside of serene peace,
and into my own backyard of faded memories
and finally into my body of overwhelming experiences.

I can see Freedom fly
She is beautiful in sky
I can see Freedom fly.

Untitled

Love is the most powerful thing in this Universe
Love is a bond two people have that can never be broken.
Love is a special thing to love, cherish and have respect for.
The more you Love yourself the more you love others.
If there is no love in this world, there would only be hatred.
This world is lucky we have Love.
Love comes straight from the inside of your body in the heart and
the physical emotion (the mind).
Love is butterflies in our stomachs.
The heart, throbbing nerves, sweating hands.
Making of Love. Isn't love just grand?

Patricia Star Downey

Nanuk is an Inuit Word for Bear

The nanuk was very fierce but wise.
He could hear the eagle soar above the sky,
And the fish jump within the water far below.
But someone was watching and shot the bear.
But some people say that his spirit still remains.......

Rocking Chair

I'm sitting in my rocking chair.
It's really, really fine.
What's finest of all,
Is that
I'm being me!

Elders

Ke Ke

The gracefulness
of an Elder
as he dances
through unknown
ground,
dancing in the
heat of a distant sun,
Honouring the Mother
thanking her for
the life,
the gracefulness
to the beat,
to the chant,
of a distant drum,
gracefulness forever seen
in the crevices
of my mind,
to remain
in silent pride
of an elder
who still dances
through the unknown!

The Unknown Song

The Drum beats
to my unknown song
a voice sings
my unknown tune,
my heart beats
to the tune of peace
Shadows harmonize,
Spirits are rising.
The Grandfathers dance
to my unheard song
The Buffalo rush
in an unassembled line,
the softness of an Eagle's wing
brushes past my lips
that sing a song
of Peace!

A Child of Six

It was the year of 1946

A young child stood alone
Tears streamed down her face

Beyond the trees
She saw a brick building

Children ran ahead of her
scrambled to see the lights
in the building

She lingered behind
She remembered her mother
Back in her village

It seemed so far away

Soon a nun dressed in black
took her hand and rushed
Her into the building

She cannot remember
the time spent there
She was just a number
dressed in uniform

Prayers recited in Latin
Offered before meals
After meals
Morning time and night time

Christmas brought nostalgia as
She wondered about her parents
While songs were played

'Silent Night" melodies
Into the night

Soon she will become a teen
She made some friends
Although not many

Now she spoke
The language of Boston
Rejected by her own

While she tried speaking in
her Native tongue
Her grandmother chuckled

She will become a woman soon
Having dealt with painful memories

She can sing now
The songs of her ancestors

She gained right to her place
Taking her identity back

Biographies

Kateri Akiwenzie Damm is Anishnaabe from the Chippewas of Nawash on theSaugeen Peninsula in Ontario and is of mixed Anishnaabe/Polish Canadian/Pottawotami/English descent. She lives in her community at Neyaashiinigmiing, Cape Croker Reserve. She received her Honour's B.A. in English Literature from York University in 1987 and her Master of Arts in English Literature from the University of Ottawa in 1996. *'bloodriverwoman,'* a chapbook collection of her poetry, will be released by DisOrientation Chapbooks in the autumn of 1998.

Mahara Allbrett is from the Tsleil Waututh Nation (Burrard Inlet Indian Band) in North Vancouver. She has been writing poetry since she was fifteen and was first published at sixteen. She had a book published in 1970, *Ka-la-la Poems,* has given numerous poetry readings, including two on CBC radio and received three Canada Council Awards. She had two pieces of prose published in Gatherings VII. Mahara is a Family Counsellor in private practice and facilitates workshops on a variety of topics. She had released two tapes, "Deep Relaxation" and "First Nations Sexual Abuse Survivor's Tape" and is in part time studies at the Emily Carr Institute of Art and Design. She has an 18 year old daughter, Sarain.

Shauna Atleo is Agousaht and Niska. She is 18 years old and resides in Victoria. Recently, Shauna graduated from the Aboriginal Youth Program at the Victoria Native Friendship Centre. Shauna's goal is to become a medical surgeon.

Carol Snow Moon Bachofner (Abenaki): Originally from Maine, Carol resides in California where she is founding editor of *Pulse,* an online literary magazine. Carol's poetry is widely anthologized. Her poem "Tea Time," was winner of the 1997 Jack London Award for Poetry. Her nonfiction book, *Drink From Your Own Well: a guide to richer writing* was released by Heartsounds Press in June 1998. Rated among the top five presenters at the California Writers Club's annual writers conference at Asilomar, Carol enjoys the conference and workshop setting as a way to share her passion for poetry. Carol Snow Moon Bachofner is a mentor with Wordcraft Circle of Native Writers & Storytellers. She currently serves as Vice President.

Bobby Jordan Barker: I am of Cherokee, Irish and Scottish ancestry. I am nineteen years old and currently attending Bryan Adam's High School here in Dallas, Texas working twenty-five hours a week on average, learning the language of my ancestors, and active in the community. I recently discovered my talent as an amateur writer, or rather my desire to do so, and as you can see I haven't had a great deal of time to spend on this new-found talent. I hope you can use what little I have written to benefit our culture and the community.

Tracey Bonneau: is the media arts coordinator for the Indigenous Arts Service Organization. As well as being a freelance journalist for CHBC-TV, Tracey is also an active member of the Ullus Collective, a group of technical media artists in the Okanagan Valley. Tracey's many accomplishments include an award from the 1995 Dreamspeakers Festival in Banff, for the music video Turning Earth and an environmental video which has been distributed across Canada. Most recently in partnership with the En'owkin Centre, the Penticton Indian band and the Osoyoos Indian Band, Tracey has instructed a ten week skills development training course for students in video production.

Chris Bose is a Nlaka'pamux Native, born in Merritt, BC, but considers North America home. He is a contemporary poet, and artist, in short he is a storyteller and one who plans to keep the tradition alive. In another time, he may have been a shaman, a hunter, a singer, a chief and maybe just someone writing their dreams on the rock forever. In recent years, he has travelled and toured extensively across Canada, the US and Europe and fully knows the rigours of surviving on the road. A performer at heart he has enjoyed playing his songs for crowds of upwards of four thousand (the Vogue theatre in Vancouver) to as small and intimate as coffee house setting; he has read his poetry in places as varied as local coffee houses, the Kamloops Women's Resource Centre, to educators at the Native Indian Teacher Education Program (NITEP), to university students and educators at the University College of the Cariboo (UCC) as well as opening for local Kamloops bands *Swackhammer* and *Four Corners* before crowds ranging from one hundred to four hundred people. To add to his repertoire, this past year, after one exhibition of his art at UCC, he was invited to contribute his work in a Canadian Studies textbook prepared by UCC professor Ginny Ratsoy. This is who he is, a survivor, an optimist, a father, a student, a teacher, a contributor and ultimately one who wishes to share his voice with the world.

Gord Bruyere is an Anishnabe originally from Couchiching First Nation in what is now Northwestern Ontario. He currently lives in Victoria, BC, where he pays the bills by teaching, researching and writing. He also has had poetry published in *Let the Drums be Your Heart* and in an upcoming anthology of Seventh Generation Books. He's been known to chase away his blues by wailing a few hurtin' songs and bases his personal philosophy on a combination of traditional Anishnabe spirituality and the teachings of Homer Simpson (a trickster in his own way).

Karen Coutlee is Okanagan of the Upper Nicola Band. She is the mother of one son. Karen also does Antler carving, hand-drums and rattles.

Donna Dean is a Cherokee-Irish author who lives in Washington in the United States of America. Drawing on her experiences as a naval officer, a mental health counseller, and a one hundred percent disabled veteran, she writes fiction, non-fiction and occasionally, poetry. she recently saw her book, *Warriors Without Weapons: The Victimization of Military Women*, selected and published by the Minerva Center, an educational forum for studies on women and war. She holds a doctorate in Psychology and the healing Arts, and has a significant expertise in victimization and healing.

Carolyn A. Doody is from the Tahltan Nation of Iskut, B.C. and is presently attending the N.I.T.E.P. program at the Chief Louis Centre in Kamloops, B.C.

Patricia Star Downey is an eight year old poet, whose ancesters include the Yupik Eskimo people. She has been developing a following in Vancouver, having recited her works at the Little Mountain Multicultural Picnic, the World Poetry Cafe and the University of BC Longhouse. She was also the youngest winner in the New Westminister Heritage Week for her poem, *The Great Fire*.

Connie Fife is a Cree writer from Saskatchewan. She is the author of *Beneath the Naked Sun*, a collection of her poetry. She was the co-editer of *Fireweed A Native Women's Issue*. She is currently living in Vancouver.

Jack Forbes is professor and former chair of Native American Studies at the University of California at Davis, where he has served since 1969. He is of Powhatan/Renápe, Delaware/Lenápe ancestry. He received his Ph.D from the University of Southern California in 1959. Forbes was born at Bahia de los Alamitos in Suanga (Long Beach) California in 1934. Professor Forbes has served as a Visiting Fulbright Professor at the University of Warwick, England, as the Tinbergen Chair at the Erasmus University of Rotterdam, as a Visiting Scholar at the Institute of Social Anthropology of Oxford University, and as a Visiting Professor in Literature at the University of Essex, England. His latest book *Red Blood* has been published by Theytus Books Ltd.

Sharlene Frank is an Aboriginal woman from the Comox First Nation. She is a councillor of her Nation, and works with First Nations on North Vancouver Island in regard to employment and training. Sharlene has written academically on a variety of First Nation's political and social issues, and this is her first creative story.

William George is from the Tsleil-Waututh Nation (also known as Burrard Indian Band) in North Vancouver, B.C. He presently lives in Victoria and studies at the University of Victoria. William has poems and short stories published in Anthologies and Literary Magazines such as *Let The Drums Be Your Heart*, published by Douglas and McIntyre and edited by Joel Maki; *Gatherings Journal, Volumes III, IV, V, VII,* and *VIII*.

April Hale, 17, Navajo, is from Gallup, New Mexico. She is of the Tabaaha Clan, born for the Salt Clan. April is a senior at Navajo Preparatory School in Farmington, NM where she is student body president. She is a young journalist and published poet whose fiery and energetic performances have won several Southwest Poetry Slams. She is the daughter of Geraldine King and former Navajo President Albert Hale.

Barbara-Helen Hill is a writer and storyteller from Six Nations of Grand River. She is a mother to two wonderful young men, one beautiful daughter and a grandmother to a lovely sixteen year old granddaughter. She is presently a grad student in two programs at SUNY Buffalo in Buffalo, NY. With her masters degrees in Library Sciences and Native Studies along with her work in healing and recovery she hopes to continue helping in Native communities. Her book *Shaking the Rattle: Healing the Trauma of Colonization* was published by Theytus Books Ltd. in 1996.

Nathan LaFortune is Coast Salish. He is 16 years old and resides in Victoria. Recently, Nathan graduated from the Aboriginal Youth Program at the Victoria Native Friendship Centre. Nathan loves hockey and is a dedicated athelete.

Nikki Maier is a member of the Wolf Clan, originally from the Taku River tribe in Atlin Lake, B.C. Nikki is a graduate of the En'owkin International School of Writing. She has completed her 3rd year writing studies at the University of Victoria. Nikki currently resides in the Okanagan Valley where she is completing her B.A., in addition to writing and snowboarding.

Dawn T. Maracle: I am a Mohawk of the Bay of Quinte in Tyendinaga near Belleville, Ontario. My father was of the Bear clan, and this is who I sit with. I was raised in Belleville before obtaining my Bachelor of Arts with Honours in Native Studies at Trent University, and my Bachelor of Education in the Aboriginal Teacher Education Program (ATEP) at Queen's University in Kingston. I am attending the University of Toronto (OISE) to begin my Master's in Education in Iroquois Storytelling. I have written for a number of college and university newspapers and special publications through Native Studies, and for people of colour. I recently published an article with Aboriginal Voices magazine. I have travelled in Ontario as well as to British Columbia and New York state to speak at universities and other educational institutions about Native role models, student organizations and support and issues related to storytelling.

Michelle is from Mowachat and Hesquit. She is 11 & 1/2 years old in grade 6. Michelle goes to Haahuupayak School in Port Alberni, B.C.

Henry Michell was a freelance Native correspondent for the *Lakes District News* in Burns Lake, B.C. He is currently enrolled in the Creative Writing/Visual Arts Program at the En'owkin Centre in Penticton, B.C. He belongs to the Likh Ja Bu Clan of the Lake Babine Nation in Burns Lake, B.C. The Lake Babine Nation are formally known as the Ntut'en and the Nedo'ats people, whose ancestors are originally from the village of Old Fort, B.C., which is on the shore of Babine Lake. He believes that his journey has just begun, because many of the tribes are interrelated in one form or another. He is part of the Athapascan language group, which is part of the Chippewa-Cree and the Dene Ta tribes, who originate in parts of British Columbia, Alberta, the Northwest Territories and the United States.

Charlene Linda Miller: Throughout my life I had wondered what my biological mother was like. My father told me very little. Relatives were not able to tell me much either. From what I did know—I enjoyed some of the same things she had. Recently I realized that I didn't have to look far. I looked within. My stepmother had to overcome obstacles greater than mine. She has taught me the greatest values. The value of honesty, integrity, dignity, pride, morality, trust, and both self-respect and respect for others. Her inner-strength to overcome her own obstacles has helped me with overcoming my own. I could not heal without the power of forgiveness. With forgiveness I have gained freedom from the demons within. My mom's oldest brother is Hereditory Chief of the Tanakteuk Band. Alert Bay is about 4/5 of the way up Vancouver Island, but is an island itself. I went there a short while ago and am looking forward to possibly living there in the future and learning my native tongue, *Kwakwala*. *Tanakteuk* is the English spelling of our Band. *Da'naxda'xw* is the way it is spelled in our mother tongue. I want to contribute to the community and become a mentor to our youth. Our culture is important to be passed down.

Moondancer (Dr. Francis Joseph O'Brien, Jr.) is descended from the Fortier line, among the first to settle in New France, Quebec, and inter-marry with the Native peoples. He is a tribal member of the Seaconke Tribe, Wampanoag Nation, and on the History Department Tribal Committee. He is also a member of the Dighton Intertribal Indian Council. Born and raised in Providence, Rhode Island, he is a philoso-pher, poet and defender of American Indian rights and dignity. An elect-ed member of the New York Academy of Sciences and Who's Who in the East, he graduated from Columbia University in 1980 with a Ph.D. degree, doing a dissertation on applied linguistics. He is a disabled vet-eran from the Viet Nam War Era. Moondancer makes his living as a career civil servant mathematician for The Department of Defense. Moondancer is President of the Aquidneck Indian Council, Inc., and a Researcher/Editor on The Massachusett Language Revival Program.

MariJo Moore: Author/poet/journalist MariJo Moore is of Eastern Cherokee descent and resides in the mountains of western North Carolina, where she writes a weekly column from the American Indian perspective for the Asheville Citizen Times. She is the author of *Returning To The Homeland-Cherokee Poetry and Short Stories, Stars Are Birds And Other Writings*, and *Spirit Voices Of Bones*. She was honoured with the prestigious award of North Carolina's Distinguished Woman in the Arts in 1998. Her works have appeared in numerous publications including *Indian Artist, Native Women In The Arts, Gatherings,* and *The North Carolina Literary Review*. Presently she is gathering material for an anthology of never-before published writings by North Carolina American Indians titled *Feeding The Ancient Fires*.

James Nicholas is Assin-anpis-kow-cthen-cow (Rock Cree), born and raised in Nelson House, Manitoba. He is innately aware of his "full-blood" heritage as an Indigenous North American. He can trace his fam-ily back five generations within the Woodlands, prairies and Tundra regions of Canada. He was given breath and voice through a long line of Shamans, Oraters, Trappers, Poets and Medicine Women.

Joanne Peter also known as *Gedawilzepq*, is a Gitksan mother of four young adults. She was born in Cedarvale, B.C., along side the Skeena River, across from the Seven Sisters mountains. She is *Lax Gibuu* and their crest is Grizzly Bear. She belongs, as do her children, to the *Wilp Malii*. She prides herself in being the best grizzly bear mama around. But remains humble in Terrace, B.C. Just recently becoming a proud grandmother, she bides her time tending to baby and new mother Tatiana and Harmony. Joanne is employed as the Director of the Circle of Harmony Healing Society, and has the ability to listen. She learns as well as teaches the loving methods of hugging daily. She knows that one day, her people will be free.

Dawn Karima Pettigrew holds a degree in Social Studies from Harvard University and a Master's of Fine Arts in Creative Writing, from the Ohio State University. A poet, fiction writer, singer and artist, Dawn Karima is pursuing her doctorate. A multiracial woman of Cherokee, Creek Choctaw, Chickasaw and other Native descent, she is President of Wells of Victory Ministries, Inc., which serves Native people on the Qualla Boundary reservation, North Carolina and in the Southeastern United States.

Mickie Poirier: This is my testimony. I speak from my studio in Lochaber West, Quebec. The Earth has a sacred space here; Bird Woman is the Keeper. There are others here, too. Earth Spirits and rhythms. Blue Sparks. I told *Kokum Lena that I wanted my paintings to be for healings. She said to hang my medicine wheel where I paint. I did that. Soon, a crow feather came to me. It marks West on the wheel. Then an owl feather was left for me. It marks East. Funny Crow! My wheel is flipped so crow marks West and hangs East. Owl don't mind, she just turns her head. Then Bear marked my door facing South with his paw and his nose. Big bear: black with a white throat patch. Glossy and beautiful. Then I could see. The first thing I saw was Bear with his paw on my door. Something happens now when I paint: Time is thrown away and the Spirits dance in the pigments!—making magic, making beauty, making sparks and jokes and love and fun! The magnitude of the gift makes me weep with gratitude and wonder. I wish you could see it. Sometimes I am frightened by what I see in the paintings, then the story clears and I can work on looking without flinching. Other times, the stories are indescribably funny! Or the images exquisitely beautiful. When I paint, it is my ceremony.
Note: Kokum Lena Jerome, Elder at Barrier Lake, Kokumvile, named for Lena, wrapped up that life in 1997 and went on to other things after 90-some years.

Right up to the last years, she would take to the woods for months, no matter the season, with her bit of line, a hook and knife. When she returned is when her family knew she was still alive. I honour you.

Sharron Proulx-Turner is a member of the Métis Nation of Alberta, from Mohawk, Huron, Algonquin, Ojibway, French and Irish ancestry. She is a two-spirited mother, writer and teacher who lives in Calgary, Alberta. She is currently working on her third book, editing a novel and is writer in residence with the Indigenous writers program with Absinthe Literary Society.

Janet Rogers is a self taught visual artist and writer, of Mohawk ancestry from the Six Nations territory in southern Ontario, Canada. Janet's images and writings are inspired by her experiences, spiritual beliefs and reflect a pride of her culture. She has worked as a curator, as well as a program and exhibition coordinater. Janet has exhibited extensively throughout Canada since 1991. She has also had an overseas exhibition in 1997. Janet is employed as a First Nations Teachers Assistant on Vancouver Island where she enjoys sharing stories and art lessons with Native and non-Native students.

Lillian Sam was born on April Fools Day, in the year of 1939 at Fort St. James, B. C. A poet and emerging writer, she is currently editing oral stories of the Carrier Natives in Northern B. C. Lillian attended the En'owkin International School of Writing in 1995 and in 1996. She has associated with the Nakiazdli Elders for a number of years and is interested in oral history. She comes from a rich background of hereditary chiefs and looks forward to a career in writing.

Carol Lee Sanchez is a Native New Mexican of Laguna Pueblo and Lebanese heritage. From 1976 to 1985, she was a member of the San Francisco State University faculty where she taught American Indian Studies, Ethnic Studies and Women's Studies courses and served as Chairwoman of American Indian Studies in 1979 and 1980. From July of 1976 through July of 1970 Sanchez held the position of Statewide Director of the California Poets in The Schools Program. Her poetry has been widely anthologized. Four volumes of her poetry have been published, *Conversations From The Nightmare*, 1975, *Message Bringer Woman*, 1977, *excerpts from A Mountain Climber's Handbook*, 1985 and *From Spirit to Matter*, 1997. *She Shepherd*, a chapbook, was published in 1995. Sanchez and her husband, Thomas Allen, closed their contemporary American Indian Art Gallery in Santa Barbara, California in 1989 to settle down on a farm in Pettis County in Central Missouri. She is currently involved in renovating a 95 year old Victorian farmhouse, growing vegetables, writing, painting and conducting poetry workshops with elementary students and youth organizations in nearby communities.

Cheryl Savageu's is of Abenaki and French heritage. Her second book of poetry, *Dirt Road Home*, was a finalist for the 1996 Paterson Prize. She has rrecieved Fellowships from the NEA and the Massachusetts Artists Foundation, and a Writer of the Year Award from Wordcraft Circle of Native Writers and Storytellers for her childrens book, *Muskrat Will be Swimming*.She is currently teaching at the University of New Mexico.

Strong Woman (Julianne Jennings) is a direct lineal descendent of the Massasoit. She is a member and Cultural Department Head of the Seaconke Tribe, Wampanoag Nation, and a member of the Dighton Intertribal Indian Council. Strong Woman was born in Providence, Rhode Island and raised in a secret Society of Elders where she was taught the ways of her people. As a child, she was a student at the Algonquian Indian School where she received intensive training in the Natick-Massachusett language from Chief Spotted Eagle of the Nipmuck Nation. Strong Woman is vice-president of the nonprofit corporation, Aquidneck Indian Council, Inc., and serves currently as Project Director of The Massachusett Language Revival Program. She co-authored *Understanding Algonquian Indian Words* (New England) with her husband, Moondancer. Strong Woman has received many awards of recognition for her creative work with school children. She was recently awarded the Volunteers in Newport Education (V.I.N.E.) Award. Strong Woman lives in Newport, Rhode Island with her husband Moondancer and their three children Brian, Julia and Lily.

Vera M. Wabegijig is from the Odawa-Ojibway Nations and a member of the Bear Clan. Vera has finished two years at the En'owkin International School of Writing and is continuing studies at the University of Victoria, to obtain a double major in Fine Arts and Hispanic Studies. This summer Vera is working on her first book of poetry and enjoying her time with her beautiful girl, Storm.

Jan Bourdeau Waboose: I am an Nishnawbe Ojibway from northern Ontario. I have lived on and off reserve. I have been writing from a very young age. I actually started writing at the age of 7 underneath the kitchen table. Because paper was not that available I wrote right on the wood of the table. For 10 years I worked with the Union of Ontario

Indians and the First Nations across Ontario in the field of Education and Child Welfare. Respect and appreciation of who we are as a people and our struggles yesterday and today is where I write from. Tomorrow, we will still be eternally strong. I have written and published numerous native poems. I also have written three childrens' books.

Jolene Shantelle Watts is 12 years old in Grade 6 and goes to Haahuupayak School in Port Alberni, B.C.

Theresa Watts is from the Dididaht and Tseshaht Band. She is 12 years old and in Grade 6. Theresa goes to Haahuupayak School in Port Alberni, B.C.

Gerry William: In terms of my biography, aside from the information you already possess, I am currently a sessional instructor in English, History, and Creative Writing at Nicola Valley Institute of Technology. I have been enrolled in a Ph.D. program with the Union Institute in Cincinnatti, Ohio, for the past year. As part of that program, my thesis is writing a novel based on First Contact between the north Okanagan peoples and European settlers. I should be nearing completion of the editing of that novel by next summer.

Karenne Wood is a member of the Monacan Nation, located in Virginia, in the Blue Ridge Mountains. She works for the tribe, directing a historic research project and writing grants. Her work has appeared in *Phoebe* and is forthcoming in *Feeding the Ancient Flames, an Anthology of Native Literature*. She is also studying creative writing at the University of Virginia.

Bonita Marie Voght was born on March 13, 1967 in Merritt, B.C. She is the mother of one child, a daughter, Montanna Rose. Montanna is ten years old. Bonita and Montanna reside in Merritt, B.C. Bonita is currently attending UCC, majoring in psychology. Her goals in life are to get her degrees, raise her daughter to be healthy and happy, keep on writing, and to live life to the fullest.

PRINTED AND BOUND
IN BOUCHERVILLE, QUÉBEC, CANADA
BY MARC VEILLEUX IMPRIMEUR INC.
IN SEPTEMBER, 1998